Nick had so many things to learn about Steph.

And one day he wanted to tell her about his broken engagement, but it opened too many doors right now. Later maybe, when he knew how things were going with them. Now they were friends. Friends almost too fast, and that scared him.

Her faith. The concern knotted in his mind. He liked her too much. They had things in common—the love of dogs, laughter, pride in their work—but that wasn't enough. His love for God was primary in his life, and he needed that in his marriage.

Marriage? Where did that come from? His heart had rushed past his good sense. Marriage wasn't an option until he got his act together and until he felt God's leading to a life partner. But that's what bothered him. Nick did feel something different. He sensed Steph had come into his life for a reason and for a deeper purpose. They had a comfortable relationship together already. When he dropped by, the pleasure sparked in her eyes. But he'd also seen the look of question there, too, and he longed to know what it meant.

GAIL GAYMER MARTIN

A former counselor, Gail Gaymer Martin is an award-winning author of women's fiction, romance and romantic suspense. *Groom in Training* is her forty-second published work of long fiction with three million books in print, and many of her novels have received numerous national awards. Gail is the author of twenty-five worship resource books and is the author of *Writing the Christian Romance* from Writers Digest Books. She is a cofounder of American Christian Fiction Writers.

When not behind her computer, Gail enjoys a busy life—traveling, presenting workshops at conferences, speaking at churches and libraries, and singing as a soloist, praise leader and choir member at her church, where she also plays handbells and hand chimes. She also sings with one of the finest Christian chorales in Michigan, the Detroit Lutheran Singers. Gail lives in Michigan with her husband, Bob. To learn more about her, visit her Web site at www.gailmartin.com. Write to Gail at P.O. Box 760063, Lathrup Village, MI 48076, or at authorgailmartin@aol.com. She enjoys hearing from readers.

Groom in Training
Gail Gaymer Martin

Steeple
Hill®

Published by Steeple Hill Books™

STEEPLE HILL BOOKS

Steeple
Hill®

Recycling programs
for this product may
not exist in your area.

ISBN-13: 978-0-373-81457-2

GROOM IN TRAINING

Copyright © 2010 by Gail Gaymer Martin

www.SteepleHill.com

Printed in U.S.A.

Rejoice with me; I have found my lost sheep.
—*Luke* 15:6

In memory of our daughter, Brenda Martin Bailey, and to our son, Dave Martin, who is the real songwriter and lead singer of Clay Adams Band.

And to Jinx, our terrier, who experienced the real two-week trek until he found his veterinarian, and we rejoiced when we brought him home. He's now in doggy heaven, but he was a character we'll never forget.

Chapter One

Hearing a ruckus in the backyard, Steph leaped from the kitchen chair and darted to the patio door. She slid it open with a thud and stepped outside. "Fred. Stop."

The yips and barks split the air while Fred wagged his tail and leaped along the fence with a shaggy gray mop of a dog on the other side.

Steph's gaze shifted to a man leaning against the fence, her new neighbor she presumed. An amiable grin curved his full lips, and he gazed at her with twinkling saddle-brown eyes.

"Fred. Come." She clapped her hands to get her border collie's attention. He twisted his neck, and she could see his struggle to respond to her call or to stay with his nose against the chain-link fence while his shaggy friend mesmerized him. Finally Fred bounded toward her.

Steph approached the stranger, who lifted his hand in welcome and then ran his fingers through his dark brown, wavy hair. It looked tousled and made him seem playful. As she studied his classic good looks, Fred tangled around her feet, and she nearly tripped. So did her pulse.

The stranger gestured toward Fred. "It's nice to see another dog in the neighborhood and right next door."

Steph chuckled. "Not everyone feels like that." She'd forced the levity, startled by the sensation she'd felt when she looked in his eyes. She lowered her gaze to his ring finger. Bare.

What was she thinking? Steph released a puff of air and managed to meet his gaze again.

He grinned. "I'm getting a kick out of the dogs."

"I noticed." His warm smile heated her face.

He grasped the fence rail and tilted back on his heels. She watched as he lowered his body to the fence again, as if thinking of what to say next. She forced her focus away from his arms.

He straightened. "I hope I didn't disturb you."

"You didn't disturb me at all." Not true. His beautiful eyes disturbed her. "But Fred and his furry friend did." Furry friend? She cringed listening to herself. She sounded like an idiot.

"My furry friend is Suzette."

Happy to have another place to focus, she looked at the slate-gray dog, its eyes nearly covered by long silky bangs. "Nice to meet you, Suzette." Managing to get her wits under control, Steph lifted her head. "And nice to meet you, too." She extended her hand. "Stephanie Wright. Steph to my friends."

"A pleasure." He gave her fingers an easy squeeze. "Nick Davis." He smiled and tilted his head toward the dogs. "They seem to like each other. It's too bad people can't make friends that easily."

She eyed the dogs, grinning at their wagging tails and their snouts sniffing against the chain links. "You mean, as easily as rubbing our noses together?"

His grin broadened. "Sure, if we were Eskimos." He winked.

Why had she said "our" noses? Noses would have been bad enough. Feeling the heat reach her cheeks, she averted her eyes. While she grappled with her discomfort, she watched the dogs' antics. Fred appeared smitten.

When her cheeks cooled, Steph decided the dogs were safer conversation. "Your dog looks like a big rag mop. What breed is she?"

Nick's dark eyes twinkled. "A Bouvier."

"Bouvier. So that's what they look like."

He glanced over his shoulder, appearing to look for an intruder, then leaned closer as if sharing a secret. His breath whispered against her cheek. "If you ask my brother her breed, he'd tell you Suzette is a Bouvier des Flandres. She's actually Martin's dog." He drew back, giving her a crooked grin. "Martin thinks it sounds classier."

"Well, la-di-da." La-di-da? Get a grip. She had to stop herself from rolling her eyes. "Fred's just a border collie from Michigan." Steph hoped she sounded sane.

"But a very nice one, I'm sure."

He'd ignored her lunacy or else didn't notice. That made her feel better.

"Martin's pitiful with his pretentiousness at times. I don't know where he gets it."

Steph appreciated the distraction. "I'd like to strangle my brother once in a while." More often than she wanted to remember. He'd upset her much too often. "My parents were thrilled to finally have a son to carry on the family name, and Hal knew it. He seemed to think he'd been born with a crown, and he expected us to bow to his every need."

She peered at Fred, his tail slapping against the grass. "Fred usually doesn't carry on like that. He's used to being around other dogs."

"Suzette's a flirt." Nick flashed Steph a grin, then crouched down and put his finger through the chain link. "Is she playing with your heart, old man?"

Fred gave his finger a sniff and then swiped it with his tongue.

Suzette had no intention of being outdone. She

wiggled between Fred and Nick, then nuzzled her nose against the links. Nick petted her, then looked up at Steph. "If you're not familiar with a Bouvier, feel her coat."

Steph leaned over the fence and drew her hand across the dog's fur. "She's not a rag mop at all. She feels like chenille."

He ran his fingers through her coat, too, their hands brushing against each other's, and when he rose, they stood eye to eye.

Something happened. Her stomach flipped, and she felt out of control. Steph motioned toward the patio door. "It's been nice, but I need to get inside. This is housework day for me."

His lips curved to a teasing frown. "That doesn't sound like fun." He shoved his hand into his pocket. "It's been nice talking with you, Steph." His brow arched. "I hope it's okay to call you that."

"Consider yourself a friend."

"I'd like that." He took a step backward. "Maybe we could walk the dogs one day. They seem to get along well."

Her stomach shot to her chest, and her response followed at the same speed. "We have a park nearby." She swung her hand in that direction. "That would be fun."

He stepped back. "Great. I'll talk with you

again." He backed away, then pivoted and headed toward the house with Suzette bouncing beside him.

Fred let out a whimper and so did Steph.

She made her way to the patio and through the door, then caved into the same kitchen chair she'd been sitting on before the distraction. She'd flirted with the man. Flirting wasn't her style, and on top of it, she'd talked about rubbing noses. Where did that come from?

Steph rolled her eyes as she got up and opened the refrigerator. She pulled out a soft drink, snapped the tab and took a swallow before leaning against the kitchen counter. She'd been a widow four years, and as time passed, she'd decided relationships were too difficult. Before he'd died, Doug had drifted from her like bubbles on the wind. She reached out to grasp him, and he vanished. Her life became dark, but these past years, she'd finally found the light. Artificial light sometimes, but she'd learned to keep her eyes wide-open. Today she'd squinted and look what happened.

Steph pulled her spine from the counter and grasped the dust cloth and lemony spray. Back to work and forget the few moments of backyard fantasy. Reality made more sense.

Nick stood inside the house and gazed through the window at Steph as she strode toward her patio door. Her straight blond hair whisked against her shoulders. The woman put a grin on his face. She loved that dog. Fred. The name gave him a chuckle. The border collie seemed well behaved and friendly. So did Steph. His mouth pulled to a grin again.

He rested his hand on the windowsill as he watched Fred trot beside her. Steph's large blue eyes, canopied by long lashes, reminded him of a summer sky. He'd been drawn to her blunt comments, especially the witty ones that made him smile. And she'd flirted, but in a nice way. She'd even flushed. His pulse heightened, picturing her playfulness.

The garage door rumbled and dragged him from his thoughts. Nick heard a car door slam. Then the garage door closed and he listened for his brother's footsteps.

Martin came through the doorway with a puzzled look. "What are you doing here?

"Want me to leave?" Nick didn't wait for an answer. He opened the refrigerator and gazed inside.

"You can't afford your own food with that business of yours?"

Nick's back stiffened. When it came to his business, Martin's humor grated on his nerves. He forced himself to let it go, then faced his brother. "You asked me to drop by to walk your dog and feed her because you're too busy. Now you begrudge me a drink?" He pulled out a cola and popped the tab. "I stopped by to offer my service."

"Service?" Distrust grew on Martin's face.

Nick motioned toward the boxes. "Thought I'd help you unpack."

His chin raised as he eyed Nick. "Unpack? Why?"

"Why not? If you tell me where you want things, I'll unpack some of the cartons or they'll be there forever."

A questioning look filled Martin's face. "You're not looking for a handout?"

"No handouts." The reference stabbed Nick in the gut. He'd never asked Martin for anything, and he never would.

"You really want to unpack boxes? Are you sure?"

"Positive."

The response relaxed Martin's expression. He tilted his head toward the largest stack of cartons. "I guess you can start over there."

Nick had stretched the truth a bit. Not that he hadn't planned to help, but his offer was the way to a means. He needed to work it into the conversation without making a big deal out of it although it was to him. He could ask point-blank, but he preferred to ease it in. Martin enjoyed pointing out his guilt.

He hoisted a heavy box onto the table and flipped open the lid. "By the way, I met your neighbor."

Martin grunted.

"She's very nice."

"She?" Martin arched an eyebrow.

Nick nodded. "Good sense of humor. Attractive."

"What does that mean?" Martin's voice left no question that he was aggravated.

Nick swiveled. "It means she's a pretty woman." Pretty wasn't the half of it. She was great looking. "And she likes dogs."

A dark frown filled Martin's face. "I hope you're not matchmaking."

"You're kidding? I wouldn't put a lovely woman through that." Nick had tried to sound lighthearted.

"Glad to hear it."

Nick avoided looking in Martin's direction. His brother would see the truth in his eyes. He'd been drawn to Steph from the moment he watched her march across the grass, and the more he thought about it, an unsettled feeling rocked in his stomach. Nick dug deeper into the box.

The rustle of packing material quieted, and their conversation ended until Martin blurted into the silence. "What makes you think this woman likes dogs?"

"She owns a border collie."

"Seems like everyone owns some kind of mutt." Irritation weighted Martin's voice.

"Attitude. Attitude, bro. Suzette's not the only dog in the world." Steph's spoiled brother had nothing on the Bouvier. Suzette also wore a crown in Martin's eyes. Nick pulled out more packing material from the box. "He might not be as classy, but he's a well-trained dog. That's more than I can say about Suzette."

Martin spun around to face him, but Nick refused to back off. "The border collie's friendly. Give him a chance. I know how you are."

"I don't want him getting friendly with Suzette. She's purebred."

Despite his provocation, Nick tried to cover his grin, thinking of Steph's "la-di-da" comment.

Rather than start a quarrel, Nick didn't respond. "Where do you want the china dinnerware?"

Martin didn't speak but motioned to a cabinet.

Nick opened the door, then lifted an octagonal plate with a bamboo shaped edge and slid it onto a shelf. Expensive he could tell. He grabbed another and flipped it over. Royal Signet China. Nick never heard of it, but he knew Martin's taste.

His own taste raised in question. What had happened to him? He'd never cared about fancy china or expensive crystal. Women often fussed about that, he remembered. What kind of tableware did Steph own? What difference did it make? He'd never see it.

He emptied the box, then slapped the lid closed. He'd already experienced one fiancée who tossed her ring in his face just before the wedding. Why would he allow himself to even daydream about another?

The memory triggered a new question. He paused until he got Martin's attention. "Have you ever thought about dating again?"

Martin's head drew back. "Me?"

"You're the only other person in the room." Nick stood with his hand on the box lid. Martin's social life ended after his failed marriage. He'd never been one to hang out with friends, and Nick didn't recall Martin dating anyone other than the woman he'd married.

"Why would I date?"

"You have a good life. You have a new home that's too big for even one person."

"One person and a dog."

"Okay, and a dog." A stream of air burst from his nose. "I just wondered. You're still young enough. You've been divorced for—"

"Don't bring that up."

Nick drew in a breath. "You have lots of things going for you, but for some reason, you aren't happy."

"I'm happy." Martin spun around, pointing his index finger at him. "And what about you? I don't see you with a social life to brag about."

His brother had nailed him. But Nick had an excuse. The business took a lot of time and money. Nick faltered. That was an excuse. He'd avoided commitment since his failed engagement. Maybe dating would work without marriage as an option. He wondered about Steph's situation. She was single, he assumed. He'd noticed she didn't wear a ring, and she'd even flirted a little. But that didn't mean much in today's society.

Nick opened another carton and removed layers of Bubble Wrap. When he looked inside, he caught his breath. He grasped a crystal plate as memories flooded back. He drew out a faceted crystal bowl, and beside it, he recognized other pieces from his youth. "These were Mother's." Sadness washed over him, picturing his mom since the stroke.

Martin glanced up and nodded. "You took some of her dishes, didn't you?"

"A few things."

Tension grew on his brother's face.

"I'm not challenging the pieces you have, Martin. You use them more than I would."

His brother gave a shrug and lifted another box from the floor.

The door had been opened to his true purpose for dropping by. Feeling the weight of his question, Nick managed to form the words. "Have you talked with her?"

"By her, you mean Mom?"

The question was moot. Nick didn't answer.

"I've talked *to* her. She can't utter a thing that

makes sense." He turned from the carton and leaned against the counter, his eyes piercing Nick's. "You're avoiding her."

The words lashed Nick like a whip. "I'm not avoiding her. It kills me to see her so helpless."

"You don't think it kills me? Ignoring her doesn't help. Do you think I don't have to force myself to visit her in that condition and fill the time with one-sided conversation? You can't shun her. She's still your mother."

"I know. I know." Nick blocked his ears from Martin's accusations. "I visit."

"When was the last time?"

Like a punch in the stomach, Martin's question knocked the wind out of Nick. "I'll go. I just wondered if there's any improvement."

"Not much. She tries to talk, but it's nearly impossible to understand her. The nurses do a better job than I do."

Knots twisted in Nick's chest. His mother was a good woman, and the horrible stroke had taken away her identity. She couldn't do much for herself. She lay there being fed and diapered like a baby. The image tore at him.

"I'll go this week. I promise."

Martin focused sad eyes on him. "It's not easy, Nick. At least make an effort."

Nick nodded but couldn't control a rebuttal.

"And will you make an effort to be genial to Steph and Fred?"

Martin frowned. "Fred? Is that her husband?" He flashed an accusing look. "I thought you had your eye on the woman."

Heat boiled in Nick's chest. "Fred's the dog, and since when do I get involved with married women?"

"That doesn't stop some people. It didn't slow down Denise."

Nick's anger softened. "I'm sorry, Martin. Denise did something terribly wrong, and I don't condone it, either."

Martin shook his head and reached for another dish. "I'm sorry for snapping."

Surprised at his brother's apology, Nick let it drop. But he couldn't forget Martin's comment about his interest in Steph. Sure, she'd gotten his attention, and he'd had fun doing a little flirting himself, but that's all it was. They'd just met. Those things happened in movies not real life.

Still his defense rose. Martin often came off badly to strangers. "Is there something wrong with being neighborly?"

Martin lowered another carton onto the counter. "I don't care what you do, but I don't have time to be hanging over the fence, making small talk. I have a business to run."

Nick took a lengthy breath and closed his

mouth. The Bible said turn the other cheek, and that's what he'd learned to do with Martin. If he knew what made his brother so one-sided, he might be able to help him.

As he delved into the next box, Nick kept silent. He'd always tried to get along with people. He'd go out of his way to be kind. Making friends only took a smile and a few kind words. Why couldn't Martin do that?

Nick closed his eyes picturing the dogs bounding back and forth along the fence and brushing their noses together, bonding a new friendship, but the dogs faded. In their place, Steph's image filled his mind, and he tried to block it. Why think about a hopeless situation? Relationships took time. That's why Martin's business was over the top while his was creeping on all fours.

Nick drew in a deep breath. He didn't have time for a woman in his life now. Maybe never.

His heart skipped a beat. Who was he trying to convince?

"Heel." Steph tightened the leash. Teaching Fred to stay at her side seemed her biggest challenge. And Fred's. In the yard he followed her well, but when he had free rein outside the fence, the dog's spirit grew, and he wanted to run. Once he calmed down, he'd be a winner and her friend Molly would be proud.

Steph couldn't believe Molly's wedding was so soon. Her bridesmaid dress fitting was scheduled the following week, and three weeks later, Molly would enjoy her big day.

The big day. Her own wedding sank into her thoughts. People married with great hopes and plans. She and Doug had. But something went wrong. He'd always been a little moody. She'd learned to stay out of his way at those times, but after the wedding, she had no home to run to. They shared a life, which meant she shared his emotional nosedives.

She'd urged him to see a doctor, to get help, but he was too proud, too positive that everyone else had the problem and not him. He'd almost convinced her. Maybe he had.

When she'd talked with Molly about this a couple years later, Molly told her to lean on the Lord. She didn't know the Lord, and if she had, Steph wasn't sure that even God could have helped. And if a God existed—Molly insisted He did—then why hadn't He helped her when she needed Him the most?

That's one thing she admired in Molly. She stuck to her faith, and she had an answer for everything. She'd asked Molly why God let bad things happen. Molly's answer? She told Steph two things. First God gave His children free will, and Eve used it. She ate the fruit from the tree of knowledge that brought sin and evil into the world. Steph had to agree. People often caused their own problems—their own doubts and sinful ways. Steph still couldn't decide about Molly's explanation. Why didn't the Lord stop Eve from eating the fruit if He knew everything?

Molly's explanation: God didn't want to be a puppeteer. Steph chuckled. Molly said He wanted His children to behave and love Him like a Father for who He was and not because they had no choice. After Steph thought about it, that made sense. If she ever had children, she would want them to choose to love her and not love her because they were forced.

Molly's second explanation: through difficulties people learn. They grow and strengthen. They lean on God for help, and that binds them together. That made sense, too.

Steph rubbed her head. Sometimes she'd almost wanted to read the Bible and see if Molly knew what she was talking about. Steph questioned a lot of things. Even now she questioned what she could have done to make her marriage better. She wondered if she were at fault as Doug had accused her. Maybe she should have gone for help. A counselor might have taught her how to handle Doug's moods, his anger, his—

"Fred, heel." She gave the leash a quick tug and brought him to her side, grateful he'd pulled her away from her wallowing.

Steph looked up at the summer sky, hoping Molly's wedding day would be as warm and cheerful. Weddings and funerals in the rain were terrible.

Funerals? Why did she let that slip into her mind?

Fred tugged again and jerked her forward. When Steph looked ahead, she understood Fred's motivation. Suzette. She gained momentum, pleased to see Nick at the opposite end of the leash.

Nick waved, a smile growing on his face.

Fred's enthusiasm quickened her steps even more. She waved back, and along with the leash, Steph felt her chest tighten.

"I stopped by your house to see if you wanted to walk Fred, but you weren't there."

She chuckled, watching Suzette wrap around his legs while he tried to untangle her. "That's because I was here."

He looked as good today as he did when she'd met him a few days earlier. Today he wore earth-toned colors, the collar of his sport shirt peaking above a rust-colored pullover.

"So once again, you're the dog walker."

"Always." He stood in front of her while Suzette and Fred pressed their noses together, then tugged at their restraints.

Her spirit lifted looking into his smiling eyes, but the usual caution followed. She wished her heart listened to the warning.

Nick jerked with Suzette's enthusiastic tug. He tipped his head toward the park. "Want to let the dogs run?"

The talk she'd given herself about not getting involved fluttered away. "Sure."

His face brightened as he took a step toward the grass. "Let's go."

Steph followed him, her heart and head fighting. Yes, she found him appealing, attractive even, but all the foolish emotion was fruitless. Allowing a near stranger to fill her with possibilities could only lead to heartache. At thirty-nine, she'd settled into complacent singleness. She had her home and her good job now that Molly had opened the shelter and shared the building with her. She had a companion in Fred, and she'd learned that dogs were everything a soul mate should be—faithful, devoted and filled with unconditional love.

Could a man offer her those attributes? She didn't think so.

Nick reached a bench and grasped the connection on Suzette's leash. "Do you think I'm taking a chance?"

"Does she come when you call?"

His face twisted to a crooked smile as his eyebrows

lifted. "I doubt it, but Fred does. I figure she'll follow him." Then he smiled, and her heart swayed like her grandma's rocking chair.

She grinned back, but her levity lost momentum. She wanted nothing unpleasant to happen to Suzette. She would never forgive herself, but her trust in Fred's ability to come when she called won out. With confidence, she bent and detached his leash.

Distracted by Suzette, Fred didn't move. A first for him.

"Here goes." Nick released the restraint, and Suzette tossed her head, then jogged off with Fred leaping around her as she went.

Nick gave a soft chuckle. "Men make such fools of themselves." His voice was low, almost as if he were speaking to himself.

Steph backed up and sat on the bench, keeping her eyes focused on the animals.

"So far so good," Nick said, pulling his gaze from the frolicking dogs. He sat beside her. "Have you met my brother yet?"

"No." She studied him. "Why?"

He shrugged, a shadow growing on his face. "He's not very neighborly."

"That's fine with me. I'm busy and don't have time to hang over the fence, either." She swallowed her words. "That is unless someone is leaning on it when I walk outside." She pictured his friendly smile the day they met.

His eyes brightened. "And the bright side is I'm not a cranky neighbor."

She understood the reference. "I've never had problems with a neighbor except a few complaints about my doggie day care when it was there."

"Doggie day care? You mean, there in your home?"

His questioning look made Steph wish she hadn't mentioned it. "That's what I do for a living."

His eyebrows lifted. "I'd never thought a pet day care could be so lucrative. Good for you." His gaze drifted to her house.

She cringed. "My house is paid for. When my husband died, the insurance paid it in full." The admission surprised her, and she tensed.

Nick lowered his eyes. "Sorry. I didn't realize—"

"You didn't know."

His demeanor had changed, and Steph was sorry she mentioned it at all. She'd dampened their lively conversation, and the silence became uncomfortable. "My business moved to my friend's dog shelter facility, Time for Paws, spelled P-A-W-S. It's nice there. More room."

"Cute name." Nick slipped his arm behind her along the bench.

Feeling his closeness, Steph's mind raced, trying

to keep the conversation flowing. "What do you do for a living?"

"I own a small company that produces parts for industrial tools."

Owns a company. So out of her league. "Parts for tools? Now, that sounds lucrative."

He chuckled. "A new company takes time to grow. I worked for Martin for a while. He owns a large electronics firm, but I decided to take the big step and open my own business. It didn't sit well with my brother."

"No? I'd think he'd be pleased."

"You'd think so." He gave her a crooked smile.

In the bright sunlight, chestnut highlights glinted beneath the waves of his dark hair, cut in layers and so thick she could drown in it. She curled her fingers around the bench seat to keep herself from touching it while he watched the dogs play.

"That's a neat thing about dogs." Steph uncoiled her fingers. "We can read them because they're honest. If they like you, they wag their tails and lick your hand. If they don't, they growl and bare their teeth. You know where you stand."

"Wouldn't that be nice?"

Nick didn't look at her, but she spotted tension in his jaw.

"Once a dog is socialized, you can trust them. In life, people aren't that open. We hide a lot of things." The truth struck her hard. She'd spent much of her life hiding things about her marriage and Doug's death. She'd felt to blame no matter how she tried to convince herself otherwise.

Nick didn't speak. He continued to stare at the grass as if he were miles away. Finally he lifted his head. "You're right. It's not only Martin who reacts without making sense. We're all affected by our mistakes and experiences."

Though she didn't understand what had triggered the thought, a thread of understanding connected them.

When Steph turned her attention to Fred, her heart rose to her throat. She leaped from the bench, seeing the dogs had strayed too near the road. She clapped her hands. "Fred, come."

Fred's head snapped her way and his body followed. So did Suzette.

When he trotted to her side, she captured his collar. "That was a close one."

"I should have been watching, too." Nick clicked the leash on Suzette. "Sorry, I was distracted."

"We both were." She hooked her hand through the leash. "I should get back." This felt too good and made her uneasy. Her uplifted spirit began to droop. She headed toward the sidewalk while avoiding getting her feet tangled in the leash.

Nick fell into step beside her as his cell phone

jingled. He slipped it from a pocket and flipped it open. Hello faded to an apology. "I'm sorry, Al. I had some business and didn't realize how late it was." He tilted his wrist and eyed his watch. "I can be there in twenty minutes."

Steph hated to listen, but Nick stayed in step with her while the voice on the other end sounded unhappy.

"Can we make it another day?"

Nick's head lowered, and he kicked a stone. "Oh, I didn't know. When will you be back?"

The voice was softer so Steph didn't feel like an eavesdropper.

"Another time, then, and have a nice trip." He flipped the lid and slid the cell phone into his pocket. "I was supposed to meet a friend for dinner."

"I'm sorry, Nick. I hope you didn't let me cause you to be late."

"Not at all. Martin asked me to walk Suzette again, and I thought I could do both." He shook his head. "When I saw you, I forgot."

She suspected his friend hadn't been thrilled. "You can't do that to friends."

He released a ragged sigh. "I know. I've been told that before."

She'd wondered about him. Nick spent too much time doing his brother favors, and it seemed to affect his own life. Why did he do that? The question clogged her mind, but she kept it there and didn't ask.

"You're quiet." He plopped his hand on her shoulder.

"Busy thinking." He should do the same. "I have to do some housework today that I normally do Saturday."

"What's happening Saturday?" His voice faded, and he patted her shoulder. "Sorry. That's a personal question I shouldn't have asked."

"It's not personal." His expression confused her—curious, yet wary. "Saturday I'm spending the afternoon having a dress fitting for a wedding."

His eyes widened, and his hand slipped from her shoulder.

"Not my wedding, naturally. A friend's. She's getting married June 6. I'm a bridesmaid."

He looked embarrassed and grinned. "Sounds like fun."

Not really. She hated going dateless to a wedding. "I hope so."

His hand rose to her shoulder again and gave it a squeeze. "Oh, come on. You'll look beautiful in that gown, and you'll have a good time."

She gave a shrug and managed to grin. If she knew Nick better, he would make a good escort. Going alone was the pits. But she would survive without him. She'd been doing it for years.

They were silent, and Nick's hand slipped from her shoulder. And why hadn't he suggested taking her to the wedding?

The warmth faded, and Steph felt horribly alone.

Chapter Two

Nick sat beside his mother's bed, studying the butter colored walls with the large clock and a card with the day and date. Everything in the facility was geared for helping the elderly men and women hang on to what mental capacity they still had.

His gaze slipped to a vase of dying flowers on his mother's bed table. The signature on the card was Martin's. Nick winced, then lowered his eyes and spotted the menu sheet below it. He grasped the paper, reading the choices she would have for her next meals—meals she couldn't eat without help. He looked everywhere but at his mother. The sight broke his heart. If he had Martin's disposition, he could deal with this horrendous situation. Whenever Nick came to visit her, a lump grew in his throat so huge he thought he would choke on it.

A guttural sound caught his attention, and he

shifted toward his mother. Her glazed eyes stared at him.

"Do you want something?" Nick knew he'd never understand what she needed.

He listened to her sounds, forcing an attentive look on his face rather than the frustration he felt. She tried so hard to form words.

His pulse skipped. "Water? Do you want water?"

The expression in her eyes validated his question. He grasped the water carafe, poured a fresh glass and bent the straw. She drew in droplets of water, some running down her chin, and when she finished, he took a tissue and wiped it away while searching for conversation.

"Martin's new house is nice."

An attentive look swept over her. "I helped him put away some dishes in the kitchen." Should he or shouldn't he? He decided to go with his instinct. "I found some of your crystal. A serving bowl and some dessert plates. A sugar bowl and creamer. They took me back to when we were kids. You always used those fancy dishes for holidays, remember?" The nostalgia twisted through him. No wonder he avoided these visits.

Her foot shifted, the only one that she could move, and she nodded.

Nick caught her flicker of gratitude. "We had a good childhood, Mom." His mind flew back to his fights with Martin over toys and chicken breasts. Nick hated thighs, and he often confused one for a breast since they often looked alike to him. "Remember, Mom, when you gave up cooking whole chickens and only bought white meat?"

A grotesque sound burst from her throat until he realized she was trying to talk while laughing.

He'd made her laugh.

His stomach tightened. He had to visit more. As much as Martin irked him, his brother had been a faithful visitor, and he'd tried to motivate Nick to do the same. His glance shifted toward the vase of fading flowers. He could at least bring along a bouquet on his next visit.

Steph liked flowers. New blooms poked up from the ground in her garden. He'd noticed them though he had no idea what kind of flowers they were. Women seemed to like pretty things—flowers, sunsets, romantic movies and candlelight dinners. He'd tried to make Cara happy, but he'd failed. Time had been her complaint. He didn't give her enough time. Maybe flowers and romantic movies weren't that important. Maybe it was time? A faint shrug moved his shoulder. He had no idea what women wanted.

He wanted people to be real and truthful. Like dogs. Steph had said it the other day. Dogs wagged their tails, and he had no doubt they were content and happy. Humans weren't that easy to read.

Nick looked at his mother again. How would Steph handle the situation with his mother? Would it even be an issue for her? His mother's eyes flickered, and he realized he'd been silent too long.

He rested his hand on hers. "Martin's neighbor is very nice."

Her eyes brightened.

"She has a border collie, so Martin's worried about Suzette and the collie getting together."

Meaningless sounds came from his mother, and her bright eyes faded to frustration.

Nick patted her hand. "I know, Mom." He detested his feeling of helplessness.

"Her dog's named Fred. The two dogs rubbed noses and became fast friends." A grin sprouted on his face. He and Steph had bonded, too, minus the nose rubbing.

His mother's mouth twisted into a grimace though he suspected it was a smile. Then her head shifted a little, her gaze probing his. He guessed her question. "Yes, I like her. We've only talked a couple of times, and if I—" If I what? If ever he needed to talk to his mom, today would be it.

Her brow knitted, and Nick relaxed. "You want to know how I really feel about her."

Her face relaxed, giving him the answer. "I like

her…a lot. I don't know why. We've only met, but she gives me confidence." That was it. Confidence. Though his mother lay so near, he allowed his stream of consciousness to be spoken aloud. "When Cara broke our engagement, I felt like a failure. I hadn't understood what I'd done. I suppose I knew a little from her spiteful comments. I didn't give her enough time."

His mother's eyes searched his.

"Now my time and energy is tied up with the business, so getting involved in a relationship is useless." Or was it? "I need to understand myself before I involve anyone else in my life." Would he ever understand himself? Doubt flooded his mind.

When he looked up, moisture had collected in the corner of his mother's eye. Maybe he'd upset her with his rambling. Nick pulled another tissue from the box on her tray, wiping away the tears. This is what he couldn't handle. He patted her arm and eyed his watch. "I'd better go and let you rest."

He sensed a guilty expression spreading over his face. He couldn't hide it. "If…when I come again, can I bring you anything?" He racked his mind for something to entertain her. She had always loved to read, but she needed two hands to hold a book. "Would you like a novel on tape? I could bring you something like that?"

She gave a little shrug, and he wasn't sure if it

was a yes or no, but what he did know is he had to come back again and soon. He rose and bent to kiss her cheek. "Thanks for listening. I love you, Mom."

Sounds slipped from her lips, and he knew she'd said she loved him, too.

Nick hurried from the building, eager to breathe fresh air and wash away the scent of medicine and antiseptic. His chest weighed with emotions he didn't want to feel. Life wasn't fair. His mother had been a good woman, a faithful wife and a thoughtful mother. Why did God give her a devastating stroke?

He slid into his car, letting the thoughts settle into reason. God didn't promise a life without pain or sorrow. A Scripture slipped into his mind, something about how in our weaknesses we become more powerful, because we turn to the Lord for strength. His mother's power was her faith. One day she would be whole again in heaven.

His throat knotted. Nick grasped his own faith and sent up a prayer for the Lord to touch his weakness with greater strength. He needed to be a faithful son just as his mother had been faithful to her family—her boys—and to the Lord.

Nick flipped open his cell phone and hit his brother's stored number. He'd nearly hung up before Martin finally answered.

"I'm leaving the nursing home now. Mom's

good. I talked about a few things—when we were kids. She even laughed. At least, I think that's what it was."

"I know it's difficult, but you did the right thing. I'm glad you went." Martin's voice sounded different—less critical and more accepting.

"I am, too." Martin's reaction punctuated Nick's decision to be a better son.

He said goodbye and flipped the lid on his cell phone. Why couldn't he and Martin talk like that about everything? He needed to pray for Martin and for their relationship. One of these days, his brother would be the only family he had left.

A lump formed in his throat, and he tossed the cell on the passenger seat. Emotions. He hated them.

Fred's bark zapped Steph to action. She dashed to the patio door, hoping she'd find Nick at the fence, but when her foot hit the flagstone, her stomach spiraled. Martin. Though he appeared to be an older version of Nick, his expression showed no relationship. Nick had warned her.

She drew up her shoulders and marched to the fence. "What's the problem?"

"Keep your mongrel away from my dog."

Steph winced and drew back from his index finger aiming at her nose. "The dog has every right to be in his own yard."

"You think so?" His accusing finger swung toward the fence.

She eyed the pile of dirt where Fred had begun to dig. Her nerves tingled, and she feared she couldn't get out the words. "I guarantee it won't happen ag—"

"Why not? You think that mutt's going to forget how to dig?"

This wasn't the way she wanted to meet Martin. And it wasn't like Fred. She shifted her gaze from Martin's mottled face to Suzette bounding around the yard as if showing off for poor Fred. He was smitten.

She sent Martin a piercing look, hoping to convince him she wasn't going to put up with his insults. "Calm down, please. Fred didn't get into your yard. He only dug a little hole."

"Because I stopped him. Next time, I might not be that—"

"Next time? I told you it won't happen again." Today she understood Nick's concern.

As her words charged across the fence, she spotted Nick racing toward them with the expression of a fireman heading for a five alarm fire.

Martin raised his fist. "He better not or—"

"Whoa, bro." Nick skidded to his side and grabbed Martin's knotted fingers. "What's going on?" He shifted his gaze from his brother to Steph and gave her one of those I-told-you-so looks.

Martin snatched away his hand.

"What happened?" Nick asked, shaking his head.

She gave a halfhearted shrug. "Fred dug a minute hole beside the fence and—"

"No need to explain." Nick eyed Suzette, prancing at his side, and brushed his hand over her fur. "Suzette, are you getting in trouble?"

Martin's look pierced Nick. "What do you mean Suzette? She didn't dig the hole."

"Martin, the dogs are getting along fine. You're the one with the problem. Learn something from your dog."

Martin's nostrils flared. "This isn't your business." He spun on his heel and marched away from the fence with Suzette pattering alongside him.

Steph remained quiet. She had to live next door to the man.

Nick rested his elbow on the fence post. "Sorry about that. Like I told you, my brother has a short fuse sometimes. He needs to learn a little diplomacy."

"That's not all he needs to learn." Steph arched a brow. "He called Fred a mongrel." She gazed into the large yard, noticing Suzette had gone inside. Not by choice, she was sure.

He leaned over the fence and eyed the hole, grasped the fence post and flung himself over the top rail, then wrapped a comforting arm around her shoulder. "I can't believe my brother made a fuss over this."

Steph's chest hummed.

His arm slipped away, and she stood dumbfounded, admiring his muscular arms while he eyed the hole. Her body ached to be back in his embrace. When her pulse stopped racing, she could finally concentrate. "This isn't like Fred at all."

"Remember, men do crazy things around women." He grinned at her before turning his attention to the fence.

Didn't he think jumping over a fence was crazy? Her mouth curved to a grin.

"Do you think we should do something to stop him from digging?" He looked at her flower beds, the fresh blooms peeking up from the ground. "Some kind of safeguard."

Safeguard? She needed to safeguard herself from her emotions. "Thanks, but it's not your problem." She plucked lint from her sweater. "How can two men from the same family be so different? Was your brother adopted?"

Nick tossed his head back, chuckling. "I've wondered that myself."

A giddy feeling came over her, and she sensed the expression had bonded to her face.

"Every time I meet you I like you more and

more." His eyes glinted as he gave her another one-armed squeeze.

"Thanks." The touch swept to her toes. She lowered her gaze, needing to turn the subject away from her. "I don't know what got into Fred."

"Males can be impetuous when it comes to the fairer sex." He lowered his arm as if he had just noticed the hug. "I'd better get inside and deal with the 'wrath of Martin.' I'll do what I can to talk sense into him, and let me know if I can help."

She doubted if that were possible now that she'd witnessed Martin in action.

He catapulted over the fence again, sent her a smile and headed toward the house.

Steph caught her breath. She loved his smile, but the whole situation gave her an unsettling feeling. She turned her attention back to the hole and kicked back the dirt. Frowning at Fred, she forced his nose to the fresh earth and gave him a stern look. "No. No digging."

She waited a moment to let her reprimand sink in, then crouched beside him. "You have to be good. I can't deal with a cranky neighbor." Steph petted his black-and-white coat as she leaned toward his ear. "Just ignore Suzette. You're too good for her anyway. She is a flirt."

Fred tilted his head, his tongue dangling, and panted as if he'd run a race.

"Let's go inside." Steph rose and slapped her thigh. "Come."

Realizing Suzette wasn't the only one flirting lately, Steph shook her head and stepped toward the house with Fred following the way she'd trained him. Inside, she tossed him a treat, then grabbed a cookie for herself and sank into the nearest kitchen chair.

Today from watching their interaction, she couldn't decide why these men lived together. They were so different. But it didn't matter. She liked the idea that Nick was close by. He could be the buffer between her and his brother. Steph grinned thinking about the way he tried to handle the situation with humor. He'd wasted his effort. Steph leaned back, picturing Nick's glinting eyes and playful smile. He said he liked her. She should have been honest and admitted she liked him, too. Too late now for should haves. She admired people who were straightforward. Being more direct with people was easier when she knew them well, like Molly, but Nick didn't fit that category.

Probably for the best.

Now that Martin had become her neighbor, she was extra grateful for Time for Paws with its large indoor and outdoor areas for her dogs, which worked so much better than her house. The move gave her ample room to care for more pets on a daily basis. Along with space, the added income made a huge difference in keeping up her expenses.

Instead of dwelling on the day care, Steph turned to the problem at hand. Fred was her dog. He lived there, and he had every right to play in the backyard. Steph nibbled on the cookie as she reviewed her conversation with Martin. He insulted her and her dog with his name-calling. When she put Martin's anger into perspective, it seemed like a fly speck in relationship to much of her life when she'd had to rescue herself. Dodging her memories, Steph pulled herself back to resolve the immediate situation.

She could take a different tack. Next time she spoke with Martin she would say nice things about Suzette and agree that she was special. Not that Fred wasn't. But he had to stop digging. Being around other dogs was nothing new to Fred. He'd enjoyed playing with the ones she cared for each day. So why now? Maybe Nick had hit on it. Fred wanted to play. So did Suzette. Eventually the dogs would be so familiar with each other the excitement would fade. No more digging.

But could she convince Martin the ogre to give it a try? If she couldn't, she could count on Nick. His charm could win over anyone.

Steph stood back, her eyes brimming with tears. "Molly, you look gorgeous."

Her friend peered at her through the boutique mirror. "You think Brent will like it?"

Fighting back her own emotion, Steph drew up her shoulders. "No, he won't like it."

Molly spun around, her wedding gown twisted around her body. "No?"

"He'll love it, Molly. You look amazing."

Molly gazed at the dress, a satin gown with hints of delicate pink blossoms embroidered on the sheer overlay. A satin bow adorned the fitted waist and flowed to the ground.

Seeing Molly's wedding dress pierced Steph's memory. For her own winter wedding, she'd worn satin with lace detailing. She'd been filled with so much hope. "The dress is perfect for a spring wedding." Steph approached her, the chiffon of her gown swishing at her feet. The soft coral shade flashed in the mirror. "Look how your veil has the same lacy detail. It's perfect. You look beautiful."

"I don't feel like it. I'm getting nervous."

"All brides feel that way." Her mind flew back, reliving her rankled nerves as she approached her wedding day, but using herself as an example wouldn't soothe Molly's tension. "When you walk down the aisle and look into Brent's face, your anxiety will be gone."

"I know, but I want everything to be perfect."

"There you go, Moll. Still looking for perfection."

Molly shrugged, and they both laughed.

Steph had never known anyone besides Molly who wanted her life to be flawless. Life did have imperfections. She closed her mouth, unwilling to muffle Molly's happiness. "Being a bride is like falling in love. You feel giddy one minute and question yourself the next. Your pulse throbs, and your chest presses against your heart, and you—"

"Hold it." Molly lifted the hem of her gown and rushed to her side, letting the lacy hem fall to the carpet.

Steph tried to read her mind. "What?"

Molly narrowed her eyes. "Don't tell me. I can't believe it."

"Okay, I won't tell you." She had no idea what Molly was talking about.

"You're in love."

A grasp escaped her. "In love?" Steph nearly choked on the word. She couldn't be in love. In like, maybe, or infatuated. That was different than real love.

"It's that guy you told me about. Your new neighbor." She moved closer, her eyes wide. "You haven't told me a thing."

"Nothing to tell." Her heart sang as images of Nick swept through her mind, but saying it aloud made it too real. "You have romance on your mind. Let's get these dresses off and have lunch like we planned."

Molly rested her fingers against her cheeks. "Steph, I miss our talks."

So did Steph. Since Brent had come into Molly's life, her life had changed, too. Between the shelter and Brent, Steph had taken a backseat. Resentment didn't enter into it, only disappointment. And only for herself. Steph's chest weighed with selfish thoughts until she cast them away, wanting only the best for Molly. "We see each other at work. We still talk." But they both knew it wasn't the same.

Color pooled on Molly's face. "It's hard to believe the date is almost here. I'd been certain for so long that I would never marry."

"That's something we used to have in common." Steph tried to sound lighthearted, but she feared she failed.

"I know." Molly's excitement faded.

Steph wished she'd kept her mouth shut. "Don't feel bad. I'm happy for you, Molly, and I've never seen you happier." She'd finally spoken the truth, and the tension lifted.

Molly eased to Steph's side. "It just goes to prove that what we think and what God has in store don't always go hand in hand." She squeezed Steph's arm. "You don't know what He has planned for you."

Molly and God. Steph wished she had the kind of confidence that Molly had.

A grin grew on Molly's face. "Now, lest you think I've forgotten what we were talking about, I'm not moving until you tell me everything."

"I have nothing to tell even if we can stay here all day." Steph glanced toward the doorway, hoping the tailor would return to break into their conversation. "It's a standoff. I'm hungry, and you promised me lunch, but I'm not going with you in that gown." Gooseflesh rose on her arms. Talk to her. Don't be stupid. But Steph couldn't open her mouth. "You're making a big deal out of nothing." Her chest squeezed.

"Let me be the judge." Molly folded her arms across her chest, resembling a bailiff in a wedding dress.

The picture made Steph laugh. "Okay, but let's get our clothes on so we can leave. The dresses fit."

"What's his name? You never told me."

"Nick. Nick Davis."

Molly's forehead wrinkled. "Nick Davis." She pressed her index finger to her lips, then shook her head. "I've heard his name somewhere. Maybe Brent knows him." She reached back for the zipper.

"Let me help you." Steph turned her around, hoping the zipper would bring an end to the conversation.

But Molly twisted her neck and spoke over her shoulder. "Have you been on a date with him?"

A date? Steph was glad Molly couldn't see her face. "If you call walking the dogs a date, yes."

Molly slipped her arms from the gown. "Does he like you?"

"Yes, as a friend, but that's fine. I'm not ready for anything serious." Her mind flooded with dark thoughts. "First I have to learn to be more attentive to—"

"Stop blaming yourself, Steph." The gown slipped from Molly's body and pooled on the white cloth beneath her feet as she spun to face her. "Suicide is a selfish act. It leaves people asking themselves forever what they did wrong and what they might have done to make it better. Doug wanted to die for his own reason. You didn't. You want to live, and it's about time you did."

Steph pressed the phone against her ear. Her fingers knotted around the receiver, and she forced her voice to sound normal, but tension had risen like a tsunami. "Why are you still living with Dad anyway, Hal? You two never got along."

"That was before. We've been getting along until recently."

She heard something in her brother's voice that didn't connect. Hal and her dad had a different set of ethics and values. They never were compatible. "What's happened now?"

He didn't respond.

"Are you working?" Steph pursed her lips, waiting to see how he'd wiggle out of that question.

"Why does everything revolve around that?"

A deep breath rattled through her lungs. "Answer me. Are you living off Dad again?"

"I don't like your attitude, Steph. We haven't talked in a long time. You're my sister. I just called to see how you're doing. I miss you."

Since when? "I'm okay."

"I thought maybe I'd come your way. You know, give Dad a few days' break. Maybe then we'll see eye to eye when I get back."

She doubted that. Forget seeing eye to eye; her father probably preferred to see Hal's hand with a paycheck. "Hal, I think before you visit anyone, you should spend time looking for work."

"You don't sound very—"

She lost the end of his sentence when the doorbell rang. Fred let out a yip as he scrambled to the door, flipping a scatter rug across the kitchen floor. "Hal, someone's at the door. Hang on."

Steph set the phone on the counter, wishing she'd said she was hanging up. As she approached the door, Fred tripped her, and she shot across the entry, one foot splaying on the hardwood and the other lifting in the air like a hornpiper's jig. She whacked against the door, cringed and flung it open.

Nick's mouth gaped. "Are you okay?"

She tried to grin, but she was sure it was a grimace. She beckoned him in. "My brother's on the phone." She headed back to the kitchen, keeping her eye out for Fred, with no need. She could hear him prancing around Nick's legs near the door.

"Sorry, Hal. A neighbor dropped by."

His deep sigh cut through the line. Steph listened to the silence, waiting.

"I'd better let you go. You have company."

Her chest filled with air and she released it in one long stream. "All right, Hal, and good luck finding a job." Her frustration had to be evident.

When she pulled the telephone from her ear, his last words struck her before she disconnected.

"I'll see you soon."

See her soon? She couldn't believe it. He hadn't heard a word she'd said. When she turned, Nick stood in the kitchen doorway.

"Bad news?"

She forced her mouth into a pleasant expression. Nick looked great. The May sun had deepened his skin tone to a bronze tan, making his chiseled features even more attractive. "My brother called. He wants to come for a visit, but I know he wants a handout. That's the only reason he'd come here."

"If you're having company, I can leave anytime if you have things to do."

"He's not coming today."

He eyed her, and she sensed he was waiting for an explanation.

"He doesn't live in Michigan." She grew silent, thinking about Hal and what he wanted.

Nick remained quiet for a moment and studied her. "You're absorbed in something."

"Thinking about my brother. I wish I knew what's going on."

"Has he wanted a handout before?"

Memories flooded Steph—times when she convinced Doug to bail him out of a problem and other times she slipped him money rather than ask Doug. That was when she had money to squander. Hal's loans were really handouts.

"I didn't mean to meddle."

Nick's voice cut through her thoughts. His face filled with concern.

The look squeezed against her heart. "You're not meddling. It's nice to have someone to talk with." She'd talked with Molly so often about her problems, the kind of fun talking like they'd done earlier that day. She winced, realizing how lonely she'd become without having Molly to herself. Today at the boutique had made the change all too vivid.

Nick was still leaning against the doorjamb, and Steph found her manners. "Let's sit." She motioned toward the living room as she moved ahead of him. "By the way, thanks for the rescue Thursday.

"You're welcome." He followed her through the archway.

She gestured toward the sofa. "I don't expect you to bail me out every time I have a run-in with Martin."

A grin brightened his face as he settled into an easy chair. "You looked as if you needed rescuing."

She curled her legs up on the sofa. "Maybe I did. I might have dug myself into a deeper hole than Fred made. With all that anger, he could have a stroke."

Nick's face blanched, and Steph knew she'd struck a negative cord. Why did she seem to say the wrong thing everywhere she went today? She'd upset Molly, too. "I'm only kidding."

"I know, but he could if he keeps it up." He fell silent a moment, then thrust his back from the cushion. "When I walked up Thursday, I could see you'd put Martin in his place. That's why he became angrier. But he needs people to talk back to him or he'll never learn." He looked uncomfortable for a moment. "I'm too close to the problem to do any good."

"I have the same situation with Hal. I'm his sister, and it's difficult being objective."

Nick gave his head a shake. "Speaking of brothers, Martin's at some kind of a shindig, and he asked me to walk Suzette. As usual, I didn't say no." He gave her a hangdog look. "So I dropped by to see if you'd like to take the dogs for a walk? We could pick up a sandwich or carryout somewhere and eat dinner in the park."

Steph weighed the possibility. "That sounds nice, Nick. I don't enjoy eating alone."

"Me, neither." His smile lit the room.

She pushed herself from the sofa. "While you go for Suzette, I'll get ready."

"It's a date," he said.

A date. Molly's question flew into her mind. Steph didn't move, watching him stride across the room to the foyer and walk out the door. Doug had been gone for over four years, and this was her first date. A sandwich in the park.

Chapter Three

Nick sat at his office desk, sorting through his mail. As he shifted the piles that needed attention to various slots, a small envelope slipped onto his desk. He placed the new mail into its box, then picked up the invitation and looked inside the envelope, recalling he'd mailed the RSVP card. He'd accepted.

Nick eyed the calendar. Brent Runyan's wedding. June 6. A jaded feeling settled in his chest. Since Cara had walked out, weddings never seemed the same. The usual joyful occasion left a bad taste in his mouth. How many weddings had he attended since that day? How much self-doubt had he pondered without an answer? What's more, he hated going to weddings alone. He felt like a drill without a bit. But excuses wouldn't cut it. He'd be there to celebrate Brent Runyan's special day. He'd been involved in business dealings with Runyan Industrial Tool Supply since he began his company. He and Brent had become more than acquaintances.

Steph's image rose in his mind. He could ask her to go to the wedding with him, but it might be too presumptuous on his part. Still…June 6. The date loomed over him, and he needed to make a decision. Wasn't that the day she already had a wedding to attend? He drew up his shoulders, guessing he wouldn't have asked her anyway.

He liked Steph. A lot. Might she be a woman who would enjoy his company without a romantic commitment? That was the only way he could handle a relationship now. She seemed receptive to talking and walking the dogs. Maybe she'd go for a casual non-date to a wedding?

A smile stole to his lips, thinking of her quirky humor and her fortitude. Martin hadn't flattened her with his overbearing manner. She'd been as strong as Martin. Nick wished he could be as resolute with Martin. And she had a heart for animals. He loved her enthusiasm when she worked with Fred or even talked about dogs.

Steph's heart was filled with kindness and goodness. The thought locked him to the spot. They'd talked about a number of things, yet he'd never heard her talk about her faith, not even a reference to church attendance or the Bible. He knew that people who didn't believe could be good people, but what about Steph? He lowered his head, admitting he'd never broached the subject.

His faith certainly wasn't perfect. His brother's, either. Martin had a devotion to things he valued— their mother, Suzette, his business. But faith? Nick wasn't certain. Martin didn't handle life as Jesus would have him do. He was too quick to anger and too unwilling to forgive. His marriage ended in a disaster, and he'd shied away from women since then. Nick questioned if his own singleness was based on the same fear. Marriage meant forever in God's eyes. Nick saw no room for a mistake.

No matter where his thoughts strayed, they kept returning to Steph. He wanted to get to know her, but he feared he had little to offer a woman right now. His business took attention, and his finances were tangled in his company. His small apartment couldn't compare to Steph's lovely house. And it was paid for, at that.

He winced. Her husband had died, then the house became hers. Not a good way to pay off a mortgage. Loss. He'd had his fill. First he'd lost his dad, and now his mother's illness left a hole in his heart. Loss didn't have a timeline. He wondered if Steph still grieved.

Nick pressed the palms of his hands into his

eyes. Why even think of getting involved with a woman in any kind of relationship. And definitely not romance. Time is what it took, and he didn't know how to use his. He'd learned that lesson from Cara. Time? He shook his head. What was he talking about? Every moment he could he found an excuse to visit Steph. Time wasn't an issue. So if he didn't want to get involved, why did he continue to pursue a friendship?

Nick drew in a deep breath, fighting his reaction—pounding heart, racing pulse, heat rising up his chest. The sensations made no sense at all. He and Steph were only acquaintances. Real friendships took years.

The phone jarred his thoughts, and he grasped the receiver. When he heard Martin's voice, his tension doubled. "What's up?"

"I'm working late. Could you drop by and check on Suzette's water and let her out before she tears up the house?"

"The dog needs training or a cage."

"Cage?" Martin's voice shot through the line. "I'm not putting her in a cage."

Nick's shoulders lifted and fell. "I'll stop by, but obedience training would be good for her. She needs—"

"I'm in a hurry. Will you or won't you help me out?"

"I said I would. Just think about what I said."

Martin muttered something and disconnected while Nick stared at the receiver, realizing the only female truly in his life at the moment was Suzette.

Fred let out an excited yip and startled Steph. "What's up with you?"

The doorbell rang, answering her question. Curious, Steph peeked out the window. No car in the driveway or in front. She shrugged and strode to the door, expecting a neighbor child soliciting for their school's fundraiser.

She swung it open and faltered.

"Hi." His broad grin caught her by surprise. "Just dropped by to see how you're fairing."

As always, her pulse skipped up her arm, and she pushed open the screen. "Would you like to come in?"

He strode in without a second thought, and she ushered him into the living room.

Steph eyed him a second. "You're not here with a subpoena, are you?"

"No subpoena." He gave her a wink. "Martin's late, and I have to run some errands so I need to let Suzette out for a run before she tears up the house."

She motioned for him to sit, and he settled into the easy chair. Today he looked amazing. He wore a sport coat—plaid in shades of brown—with khaki pants, dressier than usual, and she couldn't take her eyes off him. "You're not forgetting a meeting with someone, are you?"

A faint flush appeared on his cheeks.

"Not today. I checked my calendar." He folded his hands between his knees, and Fred took it as an invitation to sniff his fingers. Nick let him, then unfolded his hands to pet Fred.

"If he's bothering you, he'll stop if I tell him."

"He's fine." He continued stroking Fred's coat. The dog appeared in ecstasy. "Suzette should be this calm."

"She would with obedience training." She studied his face, dark eyes, almost bitter chocolate, canopied by a sweep of dark brows and hair the color of cordovan leather. When his gaze caught hers, her pulse skipped.

Nick tilted his head. "She needs it." He released a lengthy breath. "I doubt if Martin would bother."

She rolled her eyes, agreeing.

"I came to look at the fence and see what we could do." He gave Fred's head another tousle and rose.

"But Fred hasn't dug since that day. Hopefully, I won't have any more conflicts with your brother."

He grinned and motioned toward the backyard. "Let's take a look anyway."

Agreeing was easier. She enjoyed his company. Steph led him to the kitchen, then through the sliding door to the patio, hoping whatever he came up with wouldn't cost a fortune.

Nick headed to the fence. It looked different than when she'd met him two weeks earlier. The stubbled earth now sprouted colorful tulips and golden daffodils along the chain links. Since that day her life had colored as brightly.

Nick probed the ground with a piece of tree limb he'd found in the yard. "Bricks or concrete might do it. Let me see what I can do." He eyed his brother's yard, then strode along the fence to the back.

Steph assumed he was looking for places Fred had dug, but she knew her dog. Suzette had stirred up Fred that day just as Nick had affected her. The admission made her nervous. She gazed at Nick's broad shoulders as he ambled along the fence. His dark hair picked up a sheen from the sunlight, and she pictured his dark brows arching above his glinting eyes. The man lifted her up like no one had in years.

Doug's death had weighted her with guilt. What could she have done to cause him to take his own life? What could she have done to save him? Those questions had darkened her life for too long. Today she felt buoyant. Hopeful. Even though Nick could easily walk out of her life tomorrow, he'd helped her make strides. She knew now that if she could convince herself she had nothing to do with Doug's death, she could find happiness again.

"How about a high brick wall?"

Nick turned with a laugh just as Fred started barking.

Steph spun around.

The dog scampered across the yard, chasing a squirrel who dashed up her maple tree. Fred sat below while the critter chittered at him from above.

"The poor squirrel. Fred'll stay there forever if I let him." Steph clapped her hands. "Fred, come."

The dog did a double take, obviously not wanting to leave his post, but he changed his mind and trotted to Steph, his head twisting to make sure the squirrel hadn't escaped.

"Good dog." Steph patted his head, wishing she had a treat.

Nick headed toward her, his eyes no longer on the perimeter of the fence but on her. "You're right. No more digging."

"Told you."

He chucked her under the chin. "Suzette's to blame. A woman can get under a man's skin and cause him to do things he's never done before."

A man could do the same. He could burrow into a woman's heart and cause her to feel things she hadn't felt in years.

Nick rested his hand on her arm. "You have a real way with Fred."

"That's what obedience training does. It works." She hoped she made her point.

He backed up, a playful expression spreading across his face. "Yes, but does it work on you?"

"On me?" She searched his eyes.

He clapped his hands. "Steph, come."

Her feet moved toward him like a magnet. He slipped his hand on her shoulder and gave her a long look. "Good girl."

Their eyes locked. She couldn't move. She blinked, her control draining. She broke the connection, but her gaze lowered, drawn to his lips so close she could almost taste them.

"Great job." He drew back as if he'd felt the same pull of emotion. "You're almost as good as Fred."

Steph found her voice. "If that's so, then where's my treat?" Did she really say that?

His eyes flashed. "Hmm? Good question." He rested his hands on her shoulders. "Do you own a bicycle?"

Her pulse kicked. "A bicycle? I don't know if I can still ride a bicycle."

"It's like walking. Once you've learned you never forget." He squeezed her shoulder. "I can borrow one for you."

"That's my treat?"

He laughed. "It's Memorial Day this weekend

We'll go on a picnic. How about letting me grill you a steak?"

"So that's why you came over." She gave him a feeble smile as he slipped his arm around her shoulder. "I've always had a thing for steak."

"Me, too." He grew silent, looking into her eyes.

Friendship. He made a great friend, and though she could live without the steak, affection was another story.

Nick maneuvered the bike he'd borrowed for Steph into his SUV and slammed the tailgate. He eyed his watch. Late again. After slipping his cell from his pocket, he opened the driver's door with the other hand and swung into the seat. When he'd finally had the brains to ask for Steph's phone number, he put it into his cell phone, and now he pressed the memory button, shaking his head at his inconsideration. Late should have been his middle name.

The phone rang, and when he heard her voice, his chest tightened. "I know I'm late, but I'm on my way."

"I understand" is all she said, and that made him feel worse. When he'd been late for his dinner with Al, Nick knew he was irked. But Steph seemed accepting. He didn't know how to read that. Did she care enough that she forgave him, or didn't she care enough for it to make a difference?

He slipped the cell into his pocket and backed out of his garage, his mind on the day. He reviewed what he had brought for their picnic—a small grill, charcoal, steaks, bikes and soft drinks. Steph agreed to handle the rest. She was amazing.

The idea of spending the day with her made him smile. No dogs. No time pressure. Fresh air. Time to talk. That's what he needed. He had so many things to learn about her, and one day he wanted to tell her about his broken engagement, but it opened too many doors right now. Later maybe when he knew how things were going with them. Now they were friends. Friends almost too fast and that scared him.

Her faith. The concern knotted in his mind. He liked her too much. They had things in common— the love of dogs, laughter, pride in their work—but that wasn't enough. His love for God was primary in his life, and he needed that in his marriage.

Marriage. Where did that come from? His heart had rushed past his good sense. Marriage wasn't an option until he got his act together and until he felt God's leading to a life partner. But that's what bothered him. Nick did feel something different. He sensed Steph had come into his life for a reason and for a deeper purpose. They had a comfortable relationship together already. When he dropped by, the pleasure sparked in her eyes. But he'd also seen the look of question there, too, and he longed to know what it meant.

Perhaps a widow saw relationships differently. He did, though he'd never walked down the aisle. It had been so close. No matter how hard he tried to forget those feelings, they didn't vanish completely. Incidences dragged them out, making him question himself and shattering his confidence as a man worthy of a good woman. Rejection imploded the spirit, attacking trust, judgment and assurance. He'd covered his hurt for so long. On the outside, he functioned and went on.

But the inside had been shattered.

Still life went on, and Steph somehow picked up some of the pieces of his life and patched them back together without knowing it. He gazed upward at the bright blue sky—the color of her eyes—and sensed today would be special.

The drive to Steph's reminded him of too many treks to Martin's. He'd become his gofer, and though he wanted to be helpful, one day it had to stop.

Nick turned left, and in moments pulled into Steph's driveway and slipped from the SUV. Fred's nose pressed against the window welcoming him.

He strode to the doorway and rang the bell. Fred's excitement sounded through the glass but otherwise silence.

He waited.

Eyeing his watch, he calculated he'd made good time. He'd been only forty minutes late. Curious, he wandered to the backyard. No one but Fred's tail whacking the sliding patio door. Served him right. How many people had he kept waiting?

When he reversed his steps, Steph met him in front of the house, holding a picnic hamper. "Sorry. I spilled salad dressing on my clothes and had to change."

He grasped the basket, hoping she'd accepted his apology. "I was the late one." He carried the food to the car while she ran inside and came out with two lawn chairs. "I thought we might like these."

Nick nodded and tossed them inside, and they were on their way. He felt tension when he pulled onto Rochester Road, and it didn't subside until he'd crossed Square Lake Boulevard. Steph talked about her day care and her worries about her coworker Emily. He talked about his work. Neither said a word about themselves.

When he turned off University Drive to Seventh Street, he saw the entrance to Rochester Municipal Park. The fountain spilled water into the pond as they passed, and they wended their way to the picnic area. Though they hadn't been the only ones to choose this setting for a holiday celebration, Nick found a space and parked. He pointed out an empty picnic table close to a family reunion or some special occasion where balloons rimmed the area. "Okay?"

"It'll work," Steph said, grabbing the chairs and the picnic hamper while he carried the cooler.

Steph plopped the basket onto the table. "I found this old thing on a shelf in the garage. I forgot I owned it."

She'd opened the basket lid and drew out a plastic tablecloth while he hurried back for the grill, anxious to get the fire going so he had time to enjoy her company.

By the time he'd started the coals, Steph had set out a bag of chips and had settled into one of the lawn chairs. He grabbed two soft drinks and drew up beside her. The silence made him uncomfortable. Sounds from the party floated past them, and he watched the people a moment, wishing their cheerfulness would wash over him.

When their silence became unbearable, he knew he had to say something. "Great day, isn't it?" He winced at his mundane effort. He hated the distance he felt, and he definitely couldn't start blasting her with questions.

"I love it. The peace. The cheery voices over here." She motioned toward the revelers. "I've never had family relationships like that. I think I missed something."

"When I was young, we did. Aunts, uncles,

cousins. It was nice, but when we became teens that ended that."

She leaned her head back and drew in a lengthy breath. "Time moves on, and sometimes I think everyone wishes he could latch on to the moment and keep it in the present." She turned toward him. "You know what I mean? Those wonderful days when everything goes right."

He nodded, realizing that's probably what he'd tried to do for so long. "Since that's impossible, I suppose we have to make new wonderful days."

She grinned and shifted her hands from her lap to the arm of the chair.

Nick longed to weave his fingers through hers. The urge was so strong he rose and checked the coals, then returned. "A while longer."

"This is nice. No rush."

Silence again.

Nick folded his hands against his stomach and leaned back, yearning for the old comfort between them to return. Getting more edgy, he straightened in the chair. "Did your brother show up yet?"

She shook her head. "Not yet. I hate to say this, but I hope he doesn't come. I know he wants me to fix his problems, and I can't do that anymore."

Nick didn't want to ask what she meant. He tried to smooth the frown from his forehead. "You mentioned he doesn't live in Michigan."

"Right. When my parents moved to South Carolina, my brother followed. He moves with the wind—or where there's a windfall." Her back straightened, and she sounded bitter.

"And your mom?"

Her posture yielded, and she lowered her head. "She died a few years ago shortly after my parents moved south. It was sudden."

Nick's pulse skipped. His own loss remained heavy. "I'm sorry about your mom."

"Thanks. She was a good mother. No one can replace her." Despite the family struggles, Steph realized her mother had done the best she knew how. She leaned back again. "I thought my dad might come back to Michigan, but he was raised in South Carolina. He has a life there now."

"And your brother stuck around."

"When we were all grieving Mom's death, Hal moved in with Dad. But from Hal's phone call, I'm guessing Dad's ready to kick him out again."

"That's probably for the best. He needs to get his own place. I could never live with my parents. Or my brother, for that matter."

Steph bolted forward, surprise etching her face. "I thought you lived with your brother."

His back stiffened. "Not on your life. I have an apartment."

"An apartment?" She shook her head. "I assumed you lived with Martin."

"Why would you assume that?" But he knew the answer. Air rattled from his throat. "Never mind. Don't answer that." The picture flashed through his mind. "It seems like I'm there all the time, doesn't it?"

"It seems as if you're there more than he is."

He sank deeper into the chair. "You're right. He's always asking me to do something for him. For some reason, I comply. I'm like that with people. If it's something I can handle, I try to be helpful."

"That's admirable."

Though she said it, he noticed a flash of question on her face.

"Be honest. Say it." She didn't. "Don't admire me too much. I can do physical things—walk the dog, stop by the cleaners—"

"Fix a fence."

That's another thing he'd forgotten to do. He hadn't taken care of the fence. "Right."

She leaned forward, searching his face. "What can't you do?"

"I can do anything that's physical, but when it involves emo… When it hurts—"

Her eyes captured his. "You mean, you can respond to tasks and favors, but when it comes to things of the heart, you fail."

Nick felt blood drain from his body. She'd recognized it too easily. "That's one way to say it." He rested his elbows on his knee and wove his fingers in a knot, unable to look her in the eyes anymore. His mother's face hung in his thoughts. "Emotional things bother me. I hate seeing anger in Martin. I don't understand it." He glanced at her, then lowered his eyes again. "One day I want to get to the bottom of it." He started to tell her about his mother, but he hesitated. "At the same time, I don't like to see weakness in me." He gripped the chair arm, wanting to forget the conversation and just cook the steak. That's something he did well.

Steph drew back, a thoughtful expression on her face. "No one likes to admit weakness, but we're all weak at times, Nick. It's part of life." She reached over and laid her hand on his. "Men prefer action. It's natural. They like to fix things."

"I try to do what God wants me to do. The Bible says show kindness."

She stiffened and withdrew her hand. "Showing kindness sounds like a good way to behave."

Nick knew this was time to ask about her faith, but fear stopped him. Maybe he didn't want to know. "But I miss the boat too often on that one." Her expression troubled him.

"Why?"

Why? The bottom fell out of his stomach. He

could see heat waves rising from the grill, and he'd lost his appetite. "That's not easy to explain."

Steph looked uneasy. "Nick, you don't have to answer. I shouldn't have asked."

"Yes, you should." His pulsed tripped. "You said it yourself. It's nice to be open and have someone to talk with." He licked his lips. "I think the reason is when I help one person, I often disappoint someone else like the other day with Al. He's a good friend, and I stood him up."

"Because you were running Martin's errand."

He nodded, knowing he should tell her about Cara. Even his mother.

She released a lengthy breath. "It gives you something to think about." She motioned toward the grill. "I think you need to get those steaks on the grill or the coals will be out."

Nick took advantage of the suggestion. He had so many things on his mind. Food was the least of them, but this was supposed to be a holiday picnic, not a counseling session, which is what he needed. He rose and managed to smile. "How do you like your steak?"

Steph stood, too, and headed for the picnic table. "Any way you make it."

He chuckled and strode to the grill. At least he could make her a great steak.

The mood relaxed before they'd finished their

meal. Steph cleared away the food, and Nick lugged away the trash.

When he returned, he gave Steph a wink and rubbed his hands on his pant legs. "Ready for our bike ride?"

"Never." But she grinned. "I am worried I'll fall. It's been years and years—"

"Relax." He slipped behind her and massaged her shoulders. "You'll be fine."

"I will if you keep that up." She looked at him over her shoulder. "And what about my cookies? Aren't we going to have any? They're homemade."

She was stalling. "Bring them with us—and soft drinks. We'll stop along the road."

She gave in, and after he removed the bikes, they loaded their belongings back into the SUV. Nick slipped the cookies and drinks into his seat pack, and as he did, two children hurried toward them with strings of helium balloons.

"Here," the little girl said, holding up a blue balloon for him to take.

Nick's spirit warmed with the child's eagerness as he grasped the string. "What's this for?"

"For you," the boy said, and handed one to Steph.

"Thank you," she said, accepting a yellow one.

"Have fun," the girl called as they bounced away, heading for another table with the mass of colorful balloons floating above their heads.

"That's a new version of a balloon man." Nick reached for Steph's balloon. "I'll put them in the SUV, if you'd like."

"They were darling," she said, handing him hers. "I wonder why they're giving them away?"

"To make us smile," he said over his shoulder as he hurried away.

The helium made them difficult to pack away. They seemed to have a mind of their own, but Nick managed it, and when he returned, he held the bicycle for Steph. She'd worn capri pants so she had no worry about getting her pant leg caught in the chain. He remembered his mom wearing them, but she called them pedal pushers. He got a kick out of the name.

Steph mounted the bike, and he let go. She pushed herself forward with one foot and pumped the pedals. Off she went, wobbly at first, but when she stopped up ahead, she looked at him over her shoulder. "You're right. As easy as falling off a log."

He laughed at the old saying and took off on his bike. When he met her, they moved side by side and pedaled down the road.

"What's that?" Steph pointed. "It's charming."

"The Community House. It's used for banquets and wedding receptions."

"Really. It's a pretty setting."

It was. He'd seen bridal parties outside the buildings occasionally.

Once past the pavilion and tennis courts the crowd lessened. The only sound was their wheels against the bike path and a warm breeze whipping past his ears. With sixteen acres of meadows, thickets, streams and woods, Nick knew they would find a quiet place to sit and enjoy the natural setting.

They followed Paint Creek wending its way through the park, and as they rounded a bend in the road, Nick spotted a grassy area that looked inviting. He motioned to Steph and then pulled ahead of her and stopped along the trail.

She pulled up beside him, and when he looked at her, his heart soared. Her hair was windblown and curls appeared on the ends. She wore it straight, and he wondered why. He liked her golden curls. The exhilaration added a glow to her cheeks, and the sun added platinum streaks to her hair.

"That was great." Her eyes glinted. "Refreshing."

"And you thought you couldn't ride a bike."

"I'm a doubter." She turned up her nose. "I've always wanted to be like my friend Molly. She's always optimistic, and she's usually right."

Nick wished he could be more positive, too. He opened the bike pack and drew out two soft drinks, pulled the tabs and gave one to Steph. She took a long drink while he grasped the plastic bag of cookies and motioned toward the grass. "Is it damp?"

She swung her leg over the bike and strode to the

meadow, reaching down to feel the grassy area. "It's warm and dry." She sank onto the ground.

He settled beside her and unzipped the cookie bag. The scent of peanut butter and chocolate blended with the earthy aroma of the meadow and nearby thicket. As they sipped their soft drinks and nibbled on Steph's great home-baked cookies, he decided to open up the subject of his mother. Once past that issue, he could turn the conversation to Steph's faith.

Nick brushed the crumbs from his mouth, "When you talked about your mother's death earlier, I could relate to your loss."

Her lips tightened as concern grew on her face. "Your mom's gone, too?"

He looked at the ground, then pressed forward. "No, but—" He tried to form the words. "She's had a horrible stroke, and it feels like we've lost her. Her words are only a jumble. Martin's a frequent visitor, but I tend to make myself scarce." He shook his head. "I hate to admit this, but I want to be honest. That's one of those problems I mentioned. I can do things for people, but when it comes to my mom or anything that's tangled in emotion, I have to force myself to go."

Steph didn't respond at first, and Nick feared he'd made a mistake telling her.

Finally she lifted her eyes to his. "I'm trying to

wrap myself around this. Martin is a frequent visitor." She nodded as wanting him to validate what she'd said.

"Right. That's ten points for Martin. Zero for me."

She dropped back against the ground, her hands behind her head. "It's hard to picture. I would think you'd be the one to be there as much as you can."

He didn't know what to say. "You'd think." He focused on the ground and snapped off a weed, bearing a tiny white flower. "Are you disappointed?"

She studied him. "Surprised."

"Me, too. I adore my mom. But it's difficult to see her so frail and sick." He broke the stem of the weed below the flower and handed it to her. "The last time I was there I vowed I would do better. When I promise myself something, it's as if I'm promising the Lord. I know what He wants me to do."

She studied the minuscule blossom without looking at him. "It's important to visit her. You'll never forgive yourself if something should happen to her, but even more, you want to encourage her to get better. Therapy can work wonders. She needs stimulus to talk. She needs to know you care. One day you'll walk into her room, and she'll be more like the mother you used to know, not the ailing one she is now."

"Thanks, Steph. I needed to hear that." Nick pulled out another cookie, not because he was hungry, but he needed something to do with his hands. He longed to embrace her.

Silence lay heavy over them. When she sat up, he saw sadness in her eyes, and it broke his heart. "I'd love to meet your mother. I really miss mine. No one can replace her."

His chest tightened until he thought his heart would burst. "Okay."

He'd surprised her by the expression on her face. "Today?"

Today? Excuses plummeted his mind, then stopped. "Sure. That would be nice."

"We could give her the balloons."

So simple. Give her the balloons. If only he had a woman's heart. "That's a nice idea. She'd love that."

They quieted again, but this time, it was a peaceful quiet. He lowered his back to the ground as she had done.

A bird broke the silence, a melodic sound he'd heard often. A cardinal, he thought.

"Nick."

He raised his head, realizing he still held the uneaten cookie. He looked at her, and a chill shivered down his spine. "Is something wrong?" He sat up.

"Is God important to you?"

The question hit him like a sucker punch, totally unexpected and painful, because he saw doubt in her eyes. "Very."

"I thought so."

What did that mean? He studied her face, but she didn't look at him. He'd wanted to ask her about her faith, and she'd done it for him. Now he wished she hadn't. He liked her too much, and how could he continue a friendship when he knew his feelings for her were growing? The silence pressed against him. "You don't believe?"

She stared at the grass. Her eyes closed.

He wanted her to speak, to explain. "Steph."

Her head edged upward until finally their eyes met. "I don't know what I believe, Nick. I've heard you talk about God often, and I knew you were a Christian, but—" She tilted her chin upward toward the sun, as if grasping for words. "And I see things in you that I'd like to have in me."

"Things?"

"You and Molly. You both have them."

"What things?" His chest tightened until he felt he couldn't speak.

"I don't know. A joy in life. A goodness that goes beyond being calculating."

Calculating? He bit the inside of his lip, trying to understand.

"Some people do nice things so people say thank you and praise them. You don't."

A soft snort flew from him. His nice gestures seemed empty. "Steph, my nice acts aren't for a thank-you or praise. I'm driven to do them for others. It's the way I am, and it's not always good. Think of Martin and me. Neither of us is doing each other a favor."

She nodded as if she understood. "Molly's a believer, and I've asked her a million questions. Some of her answers make sense."

A sliver of hope poked through his despair. "Have you read the Bible?"

"I've thought about it, but like things we want to avoid, I don't."

His mind flew in a multitude of directions. "Why would you want to avoid it? If you're questioning, read the Word, and it will help you find answers."

Her face grew intense. "I know you can't understand, but I live in a comfortable rut. I know myself, and if I open the door to something I don't know…" Her gaze clung to his as if begging for answers. "What if I don't like the answer? What if I realize I'm doomed for the hell that Christians talk about."

"If heaven is real to us, Steph, we have to accept hell. God sent His Son so that we would have eternal life. Hell is the opposite. Not having eternal life. Not being with Jesus. It means being in—"

"The fiery furnace?"

He shook his head. "Hell is the absence of God. It's a place without hope and without love."

Tears rimmed her eyes, and he slipped closer and wrapped his arm around her shoulders not knowing how else to comfort her besides praying, and he would do that.

She leaned into him. "I've asked myself if this is all there is to life. I think about dying and just vanishing. Being dirt that fertilizes the flowers I love. It could be worse."

"But it could be so much better." He drew her closer, his hand rubbing her arm. "You are worth more. You're a child of God, but you've never met your Father."

She tilted her head and closed her eyes. "It sounds so easy, but it isn't."

The special day he'd anticipated had become special but not in the way Nick had expected. She needed time to think—and so did he. *Lord, give me words.*

Steph lifted her hand and brushed away her tears. "I'm sorry, Nick."

"Don't be sorry." He felt at a loss. "I care about you, Steph. I hope you consider us good friends. You're important to me."

Her eyes misted again. "I was afraid if you knew the truth, you wouldn't want to be my friend anymore."

He gave her a squeeze, then pushed himself up from the ground. She rose beside him, and he pulled her to his chest and held her there. He had so much to think about. So did Steph. She felt so small in his arms. He wanted to help her. He wanted to love her.

She drew away. He let her go, but his arms felt empty.

He picked up their trash, and Steph moved to her bike. They didn't speak. They pushed off, and on the way back, the only sound he heard was his heart beating in his ears.

Chapter Four

Steph found talking difficult on the way home. Her admission of not being a Christian had dampened both Nick's and her spirit, and though Nick tried to cover it by slapping a smile on his face, it didn't work. She knew him well enough to see the disappointment—even concern—in his eyes. Leaving well enough alone seemed prudent today. She needed to think, and he did, too. That's what she feared.

The Bible seemed to be an important part of faith. Molly had mentioned it so many times. It guided Molly's life. God's Word, she called it. Now Nick said the same. She released a ragged breath, and Nick glanced at her but didn't say anything.

Grateful that the drive was short, Steph worked to pump up her spirit as they approached the entrance to the rehabilitation center. She carried the balloons, and the image created a pitiful paradox in her mind. She'd become the sad-faced clown.

Nick opened the door for her, and she sent him a halfhearted grin. When she stepped inside, the pungent scent of disinfectant permeated the air. A visit that had started out filled with hope now discouraged her. At least her visit would be an act of kindness. The Bible called for people to be thoughtful.

"It's that way." Nick motioned to the corridor ahead of them. They turned, and three doors down, he stopped. "This is it."

She stood outside the doorway while he walked in. From a distance, she saw a woman who'd once been pretty. Even today, though her face had been twisted by the stroke, her eyes sparkled and her creamy skin looked like a china doll.

Nick beckoned to her, and Steph stepped inside, the balloons splashing color against the soft yellow walls. "Mom, this is Stephanie Wright. I told you about her." He turned toward her. "Steph, this is my mom, Julia Davis."

She crossed over to his mother and extended her hand before realizing her right one was paralyzed. "It's very nice to meet you." She patted Julia's arm. "Niis."

Nice. His mother had spoken. She turned to smile at Nick.

His eyes had widened like a full moon. "Mom." He moved to her side and leaned over. "I understood you. That's wonderful."

Relief flooded his face as he sank to the edge of the bed and held his mother's hand.

Julia's face settled into a lopsided smile, and she managed to move her free hand across her body and placed it over Nick's.

Steph stood back, watching the emotional connection of mother and son. Her own mother filled her memories, and tears blurred her eyes. She'd had a difficult life, but she'd tried hard to be as good as Steph's dad allowed her to be.

Nick turned to face her and grinned. "You look like a clown."

She realized she still held the balloons. A chuckle escaped her, and it felt wonderful. Her shoulders lowered as the tension eased away.

"These balloons are for you," she said, lowering the balloons. "Some children gave them to us in the park."

Julia's face brightened, obviously pleased. "Can I tie them here so you can see them?"

"Yeez."

Another word. Progress. Nick looked elated, and Steph enjoyed witnessing the special event. It soothed the stress she felt after her talk with Nick. Steph tied the balloons to a chair back close enough

for Julia to see, then settled into one of the chairs.
She listened to Nick asking about therapy and
telling her about their picnic and bike ride. He
talked about his work—something she knew little
about. He even mentioned Martin.

"Steph has a doggie day care."

Julia's twisted mouth formed a word. This one
she didn't understand. She wanted to help the frail
woman so badly—help her talk and walk again. If
Julia were her mother, she would be devoted to her
even if… She faltered. That was easy to say but
harder to do. With her day care and household
tasks, the word *devoted* didn't fit. Life marched on.
People had responsibilities. But having lost her
mother, now she'd become even more precious.

Had her mother been a believer? Maybe. Steph
remembered her going to church once in a while
when Steph had been very young. She may have
gone, too, but time passed and church attendance
faded. Her mother had dealt with a difficult life.
Steph thought about heaven. If her mother believed
then she would be in heaven.

"Don't you agree?"

Nick's voice broke into her thoughts. "Agree?"

"Suzette needs obedience training."

So did Martin. She agreed about Suzette and
gave a short pitch-talk about the training, hoping
to encourage Nick to talk with his brother.

The uncomfortable chair caused Steph to squirm. She leaned back, trying different positions, as her gaze swept the room. A bouquet of flowers stood on the windowsill. She tried to read the inscription but couldn't. A Bible lay on the stand near Julia's bed. She wondered if his mother could hold it so she could read.

"Do people read to your mother?"

Nick shifted on the edge of the bed and shrugged. "I mentioned bringing her some audio books. I haven't." He glanced at the table and picked up the Bible. "Does someone read to you, Mom?"

A flustered expression settled on Julia's face as she tried to speak. Nick watched her and then glanced at Julia, lifting his shoulder in a questioning shrug.

Steph rose and walked to the edge of the bed. "Sometimes."

His mother's head tilted.

"Not very often?"

This time she gave a full nod.

Steph's pulse kicked as she formed an idea. "I could drop by once in a while and read to you if you'd like?"

Julia's eyes sparkled. "Yeez."

"Wonderful. I love to read."

Nick's eyes filled with gratitude, and he slipped his hand in hers and squeezed. "Thank you. That would be really nice."

Steph smiled, thinking she could stop after work Tuesday and find a book Julia might enjoy.

"Bibo."

Nick's head turned, and Steph leaned forward, trying to figure out what she wanted.

Her veined hand shifted on the bed, and one finger pointed to the table.

Nick followed her movement. "Bibo?"

Steph knew, and gooseflesh rose up her arm. "She said Bible."

Nick's head pivoted toward Steph. "She wants you to read her the Bible." His eyes searched hers, a desperate look on his face.

"I know." Buzzing sounded in her ears. She sank back into the chair. God worked miracles. She'd heard that from Molly, and if she didn't know better, this could be God guiding her steps. She waited for the dizziness to pass, then drew up her shoulders. She'd questioned reading the Bible before. Now this?

Too strange. She struggled with the idea. God could do anything. That was logical, but what happened today wasn't.

"You have a call."

Steph lengthened her frame when she heard the intercom and checked on her dogs before picking up the receiver.

Nick's voice surprised her. "Sorry to call you at work."

"That's okay. His voice held an edge of concern. His mother? "Is something wrong?"

"Everything's fine."

She tried to decipher what she'd heard. Since Memorial Day, she'd anticipated Nick walking out of her life, and frustration took over. Why had she been so open about her faith? But he hadn't turned his back. She didn't know what she would have done. The thought of him vanishing from her life had ripped her apart.

"Your mother's okay?"

"She's fine. I haven't seen her since we were there."

She wanted to chastise him for not visiting. Wisdom stopped her. She'd promised to drop by, and she hadn't, either. Too many things pressed on her mind. "I thought…when I heard your voice, I feared it was bad news."

"Nothing's wrong, and thanks for worrying." His voice sounded more like the Nick she knew so well. "I'm at a building supply, checking ideas to resolve the fence issue."

The fence. She had no problem with the fence until his brother appeared in her life. The whole issue irritated her. But Nick's concern seemed so natural. "Any ideas?"

"A couple, but I want to show you first."

Again the subject of cost wavered through her stomach. "Can you pick up brochures?"

"I have some in my hand."

She pictured his tan hands with long fingers clutching the glossy pamphlets. Her fear lifted for the first time since Memorial Day. She'd wondered what her confession had done to their friendship, and if she looked in his eyes, she would know the truth. "How about dropping by here? I wanted you to see my day care and the shelter anyway."

"Works for me."

A flutter rippled in her chest. "We're on Rochester Road near—"

"I know where it is. See you in twenty minutes."

He must have checked out the building. Just like him. She peered at her watch and opened the back door, allowing the dogs to run into the yard. She stood a moment, feeling the chill of the cooler day and of her concern over seeing Nick again.

Flowers had sprouted, though many were still waiting to shoot up from the ground. Planting wasn't safe in Michigan until after Memorial Day, and even then, it wasn't a sure thing. Since her confession, her own emotions lingered like shoots beneath the ground, waiting for the sunshine of Nick's smile and the warmth of his acceptance.

After the visit with his mother, she longed to

hear him say something to give her hope, anything to let her know that his friendship hadn't been marred by her confession, but he'd talked about his mother's illness and concerns. The time wasn't right to probe him on his feelings for her, so Steph remained quiet.

A shiver ran down her back. She stepped inside, grabbed a jacket and tossed it over her shoulders. She loved watching the dogs play outside. No one bothered them. They could bark without a care in the world. If only she had the freedom, the kind that made a difference to her spirit. Molly had that freedom. Steph had always sensed it, and now she'd seen it demonstrated in Nick. She'd put a name on it.

Faith.

The word settled over her, and Steph wished she could wrap her arms around it, but she didn't know how. She knew it had to do with being saved and eternity. Often she'd wished that when life ended that was it. Nothing. She would just vanish, and all that was "her" would be no more.

But since meeting Nick, the thought scared her. She asked herself, "Is this all there is?" like the old tune she'd heard years earlier. If that was so, then what was life all about? It seemed rather futile. Sure, she'd enjoyed her work. She loved Fred. Molly. Her friends. But life seemed filled with loneliness. A solitude she didn't like.

Nick made her days different. She'd said it before, but now it had deeper meaning. After Doug died, she'd withdrawn like a turtle into her shell as far as men were concerned. But when she met Nick, her spirit lifted. She seemed to have purpose. He made life interesting. Fred had been her fun and still was, but that didn't fill her loneliness for real companionship.

Deeper than his good looks, Nick charged with thoughtfulness and confidence tied to his faith, a faith that he lived and not just talked about.

Molly always said it wasn't what was on the outside but on the inside, and Steph had begun to understand. Doug had been a great-looking guy, but on the inside, his moods and his nasty temper were troubling and destructive. Why hadn't she realized it sooner, like before they married? That's when she had gone wrong.

Steph bent her head back, taking a deep breath, grateful that she'd overcome some of the guilt and shock of her husband's suicide. Marrying again seemed as unlikely as climbing Mount Everest. She had no desire to climb anything, and she had little hope of considering a permanent relationship. But friendship. Yes, and she cherished Nick's.

Lost in thoughts, Steph jumped when Fred let out his happy bark. She stepped onto the grass and spotted Nick at the fence nuzzling Fred's head as the dog balanced on his front paws against the chain links. Her other day care dogs jigged beside Fred, wanting attention, and Nick reciprocated as he always did. He reached across and gave each dog a friendly pat.

Nick had stolen Fred's heart as he had hers.

The old fear slammed against her chest. She didn't know herself anymore. Out of her rut, she stumbled and doubted. Her decision to enjoy Nick's company without getting involved in romance burst when she saw his smiling eyes. If she could only come to grips with her past, her confidence might return. But even then, the faith issue stood as an even stronger bulwark.

Nick waved then vanished around the corner of the building.

Steph stepped inside to greet him, but the battle of head and heart came into play again. Her head screamed friendship while her heart longed to rush into his arms.

He waved the brochures. "Nick Davis to the rescue."

"Again? You're always rescuing me." Chills bristled down her spine.

"Only when you need it." He strode forward and slipped the brochures into her hand, then wrapped his arm around her shoulders as if nothing had happened between them.

She clamped her fingers over the glossy paper, confusion wavering in her mind. "Thanks. You're too thoughtful."

"A man can never be too thoughtful."

His gentleness pinged in her heart. "You're right. I like you that way."

"I like you."

Steph nearly lost it. He gave her a final squeeze and stepped away in time for her to gather her wits. She needed to back away or plunge forward, but neither worked in her situation. She owed him honesty. His faith meant too much for her to play lightly with it. Right now, she longed for something to distract her. "Want to see the shelter?"

"I'd love to."

She dropped the brochures onto her desk, checked the dogs one more time and gestured toward the doorway. "It's through there."

Her gaze swept over him again, trying to fathom what was wrong with her. She'd never reacted to any man in her life as she did with Nick. She moved on gelatin legs to the door and swung it open. With the barrier removed, dog sounds met them—toenails slipping on tile, barks of excitement, whines of curiosity.

Nick drew back. "When you say you have dogs here, you mean it." His face reflected his concern.

"You've never been to a shelter?"

He shook his head and stepped deeper inside the kennel area. The further he ambled, the more concern spread over his face. "All of these dogs need homes?"

"They do. Some aren't ready yet. They need more obedience training. We use my dog day care area in the evenings, and the smaller area back there is for our volunteers to work with them whenever they're here."

Nick moved along the small enclosures, stopping to pet the dogs as he made his way to the end. "This breaks my heart."

A knot twisted in Steph's throat. "Mine, too. Most of them will make wonderful pets."

"If no one adopts them, what happens?" He turned sad eyes toward her.

Her heart squeezed. "Don't ask."

He shook his head, a look that told her he understood.

The door at the far end of the hallway opened and Molly's new employee walked in, a curious expression on her face. "Oh." She faltered as if surprised.

"It's just me and a friend." A friend. The word caught in her throat. She moved closer. "Emily, Nick Davis." She motioned toward Nick. "Nick, this is one of our part-time employees. Emily Ireland."

They shook hands, and then Emily turned to the black-and-white terrier skittering inside the enclosure beside them. "Are you looking for a dog? This one's ready for adoption."

Nick pressed his lips together, obviously hating to tell her the truth. "No, Steph's just showing me around. I've never been here."

"Oh." Disappointment flattened her voice as she backed away. "Then I'll get back to the office. I checked because I heard voices." She gave a meager wave as she walked away.

They watched in silence as Emily passed through the doorway, then Steph rested her hand on his arm. "Don't feel badly. You have Suzette, and you're great with her. She's more your dog than Martin's any day."

"I don't know why Martin wanted a dog. I thought for companionship, but I seem to be her companion."

The door opened again, and Steph glanced up surprised to see Molly. "Why are you here already?"

Molly looked at Nick, then back at Steph. "I came in early. A new puppy arrived last night. Did you see him?"

Puppies broke her heart. "Not yet."

As it always did when a new dog arrived at the shelter, Molly's face glowed with her dream to save dogs and find them homes. "I was anxious to check on him, but he seems fine."

Steph's pulse skittered. "Molly, this is Nick Davis."

Molly's eyes lit up as she extended her hand. "Great to meet you, Nick. You're a friend of my fiancé, Brent Runyan, aren't you?"

Nick drew back, his eyes widening. "Yes. You must be Brent's Molly." He shifted his gaze from Steph back to her. "I received an invitation to your wedding."

Steph gasped before she could restrain the emotion.

Molly chuckled. "No wonder your name was so familiar when Steph mentioned you the other day."

Nick nudged Steph with his elbow. "So, you talked about me?"

Heat rose up Steph's neck. "I did." She wanted to strangle Molly, but then how did she know her statement would embarrass her?

A twinkle lit Nick's eyes. "I hope she said nice things."

Molly grinned. "Very nice."

Awkward silence settled over them, and Steph wanted it to end. She swung her arm toward the end of the hallway. "Show us the puppy."

Her shoulders eased as Molly flagged them to follow. She stopped by one of the enclosures nearest the doorway to the offices.

Steph's heart melted. "He looked like a little fluffy beige-and-white ball. He's a—"

"A cocker spaniel." Love filled Molly's eyes. She had a heart of pure goodness.

Nick rested his elbows on the half door of the pen. "Look at those rusty ears."

"Roan is the color." Molly paused, a coy look in her eyes. "I'll let you two talk. I have some paperwork to do." She took a step backward. "So nice to meet you, Nick, and I'll see you at the wedding."

"You will."

The wedding. Steph didn't move as Molly slipped through the door. Reality settled in. Nick had been invited to the wedding. She longed to suggest they go together, but she couldn't. She'd never asked a man to be her date. Never. A bridesmaid had too much responsibility anyway.

She stepped back. "I need to check on the dogs, and then I'll look at the brochures."

Nick caught her hand as she turned away. "Not so fast."

Her stomach flipped. "What?"

His eyes searched hers. "So this is the wedding you mentioned the other day."

She held her breath and nodded.

"Do you have an escort?"

Her chest pounded. Go for it, Steph. "Not really. But I'm a bridesmaid, remember? One of the groomsmen walks me down the aisle after the ceremony. That's it." Her heart pounded in her ears.

"If that's the case, I'd love to be your escort." His face broke into a smile. "I hate attending weddings alone."

For some ridiculous reason, she felt nervous. This almost seemed like a real date. "I'd love to, but you'd still be alone. I'm expected to eat at the head table, and I have to be there early. It seems—"

He touched her arm. "But I won't be alone. I'll be with you."

His smile warmed her heart, and if she'd been a person who prayed, his invitation would have been God's answer to her prayer. "If you don't mind, it would be nice."

Nice? The word meant nothing to what she really felt inside.

Nick grasped her hand and gave it squeeze. "Wonderful."

Wonderful. That was much closer to the truth.

Chapter Five

Steph stood in the doorway of Julia Davis's room. A peaceful expression gilded her face as she slept. Light streamed in from the window on a fresh display of flowers. She wandered across the tile floor and lifted the card stuck into the blossoms, expecting to see Martin's name. Her chest tightened. Nick. He'd visited.

When she lowered her eyes the sun spilled below the vase, adding a glow to the gold embossed letters on the black leather cover of the Bible. Steph placed the package she'd brought for Julia next to her feet against the chair leg, then studied the hospital-like room with today's date grafted to the wall beside the large clock so Julia could hold on to a world outside the bare walls.

Steph settled into the comfortable chair and leaned back. She closed her eyes, picturing Nick at the shelter, his compassion showing for the dogs and his excitement about being her escort at the wedding. Even the information he gave her about the fence situation seemed enthusiastic. And what had impressed her most had been his thoughtfulness about the cost. And without her needing to ask.

The supply company had suggested blocking that particular area along the fence with stones. Nick had said she could create a rock garden there, an idea she liked. Another solution was placing railroad ties at the fence bottom. Not as attractive, but possible. She could also lay chicken wire flat against the ground just under the fence and project into the flower bed so he couldn't dig. She worried about him cutting his paws no matter how careful she was.

She hadn't decided yet, probably because she didn't see it as a problem. Still Steph wanted to stay in the good graces of Nick's brother. But that wasn't her motivation. Nick's eagerness to help glowed on his face, and she hated to refuse to do anything. Lighthearted or serious, Nick had a spirit that she loved.

Her eyes shifted to the Bible, then lowered to the paperback books she'd purchased. She lifted the bag and pulled out one. She'd read the back blurb. It mentioned faith so she'd assumed it was Christian fiction. She had often thought the whole Bible was Christian fiction, but so many people she cared about believed it was truth.

Slipping the novel back into the sack, Steph set it on the floor and turned her eyes again to the Bible. Nick had been guided by that book all his life, he'd said. She hadn't, but her life wasn't over yet. She moved her hand and placed it on the leathery binding. The cover looked worn as if it had been opened and read often.

Without thought, she lifted the book from the table and held it in her hand. Julia's eyes were still closed, and Steph pondered whether to leave or wait to see if she'd waken. Her fingers trembled as she lifted the cover and scanned the books—Genesis, Exodus, Leviticus, Numbers. She closed the cover, and when she looked up, Nick's mother was watching her.

Julia moved her head, her arm inching upward. "Hello."

Steph leaned forward. "Do you remember me? I'm—"

"Nick…"

She nodded. "Yes, Nick's friend. Steph." Her palms dampened against the Bible, and she felt guilty holding it. If she could place it back on the table without being obvious, she would. "Your flowers are lovely."

Julia's mouth curved up on one side. "Nick."

"He must have visited." Trying to find conversation boggled her for a moment, and she understood how Nick must feel.

"Yes." Her eyes flashed as if she had so much to say. Instead frustration grew on her face.

Steph grabbed at any topic. "Nick's been helping me with some work along my fence."

"Nice."

The word was more distinct then when she'd been there last. "Your speech is improving. That's good news."

His mother nodded but motioned toward her arm and shook her head.

"Can you use your arm yet?"

"No." She managed a faint shrug.

"You'll get better each day with therapy." As she shifted, her foot knocked the paper bag holding the novels, and Steph bent to pick them up. "I brought you a couple of books so you can read when you're feeling better. It's Christian fiction. I thought you might like them."

Her eyes glinted as she formed a thank-you.

"Would you like me to read a little from one of them?" She set both books on the edge of the bed so she could view them.

"Bible. Read."

Bible. She looked in her lap where the book still lay and stared at it a moment. Fate or God, a power beyond her control wanted her to read this book. Molly, first. Then, Nick. Now, Julia. She lifted it and opened to the first page. Genesis. "Chapter one.

In the beginning God created the heavens and the earth. Now the earth was formless and empty—"

"No."

Steph's head shot up. "You don't want the Bible?" A mixture of emotions spiraled through her. A strange sense of disappointment had struck her rather than the relief she would have expected.

"Yes." She moved her finger upward with a wiggle.

Following the direction, Steph realized a bookmark peeked from one of the pages deep in the pages. "Here?"

Julia smiled and lowered her head.

Trying to keep her hands from shaking, Steph opened the pages at the bookmark. Formless and empty described the feelings Steph had before Nick came into her life. Not empty exactly. She had few friends, and Molly had been great company always, but empty on the inside, a drab hopeless feeling that made her yearn for something deeper.

When she glanced up, Julia was watching her with question in her eyes. "Should I begin here in 2 Corinthians?" She turned the Bible toward Julia.

She nodded.

Steph swallowed, her throat so dry it felt parched. She licked her lips and began to read. The header said the speaker was Paul. She'd heard of Paul the sinner, who became a devout and influential Christian. Molly had spoken of him. The verses talked about Moses and a veil that fell over the eyes of the people as they'd hardened their minds so they couldn't understand, but the veil could be lifted by believing in Christ.

Her tongue adhered to the roof of her mouth, but she continued. "But whenever anyone turns to the Lord, then the veil is taken away. Now, the Lord is the Spirit, and wherever the Spirit of the Lord is, he gives freedom."

Freedom. The concept tore through Steph's mind. How long had she yearned for the kind of freedom Nick had? And Molly? She forced herself to read on. "And all of us have had that veil removed so that we can be mirrors that brightly reflect the glory of the Lord." Nick's eyes. The brightness, the glint she so admired filled her thoughts. Was this God's spirit? Could it be seen? "And as the Spirit of the Lord works within us, we become more and more like him and reflect his glory even more."

The words stirred in Steph's chest. She'd seen the glow in Nick, a kind of spirit that radiated from him. Not that playful look that glinted in his eyes but a depth that made her long to be there with him.

When she looked up, Julia's eyes were closed, and she breathed softly. Steph slipped the marker between the pages, then returned the Bible to the table. She rose and stood over her, recalling her mother's face.

Julia didn't stir. Steph grasped the two novels and slid them beside the flowers. Another time for those. She looked again at Nick's mother, then tiptoed from the room.

Had she hardened her heart? No. How could she? She'd never known him. But if the veil could be lifted, maybe she would understand?

And this veil can be removed only by believing in Christ.

But how could she do that?

As she watched through the window, the mail truck passed her house, and Steph headed to the street to collect hers. She paused at the box and shuffled through the envelopes. Nothing from her dad telling her Hal was heading her way. No bills. The sun dappled the lawn as she started up the sidewalk to her door, but before she reached the porch, she heard a car door close. She turned to see Nick slipping from his car onto Martin's driveway. He took off his sport coat and tossed it on the passenger seat before he turned.

No matter how hard she tried to control her feelings, her pulse propelled when she saw him. He looked amazing as always. Today he wore khaki pants with a crisp pleat along with a claret-colored polo shirt. His well-formed lips curved to a smile.

Willing away her flustered emotions, she waved

and waited as he crossed the lawn to reach her. The idea of Nick living in an apartment and not next door still staggered her. Where he lived had never come into their conversation, and she'd assumed he lived there. He appeared to be at Martin's so often. Details weren't always as they seemed. A life lesson she needed to note.

Nick slowed as he reached her. "Thanks so much."

His smile was as sunny as the glow that lit his face. "Thanks? For what?"

He slipped his arm around her shoulders. "For visiting my mom." He drew her closer to his side. "She appreciated it so much."

A chuckle escaped her. "I put her to sleep."

He shrugged. "She sleeps a lot. It meant a great deal to her that you came." He paused, turning her to face him. "She said you read her the Bible."

Steph's breath left her for a moment. "I think I misled her." What had caused her to pick up the Bible in the first place? That had troubled her and left her with an eerie feeling as if she hadn't been in charge of her actions that day.

"Misled her? How?"

"The Bible was sitting on my lap when she woke." The image hung in her mind. "I don't know what motivated me to pick it up, but I had."

A flicker of uncertainty flashed on Nick's face.

She waited, hoping he would tell her what was on his mind.

Instead he changed the subject. "Mom's doing much better today. They're working her hard." He eyed Fred in the doorway and took a step toward him.

Steph followed. "What were you thinking, Nick?"

"About my mom?" His eyes were focused on Fred before he turned to face her. He shook his head. "That's not what you meant. You want to know what I thought about you holding the Bible."

She nodded, eager to hear his answer.

He swept his fingers through his hair. "My first reaction was relief, followed by hope."

Relief? Hope? The meaning wavered in her mind. "And the second?"

His gaze captured hers. "It was a praise of sorts. God does guide our steps."

Her chest tightened. Though her disbelief had always been unshaken, her confidence had experienced a tremor. "Our steps."

"His children's steps."

Her finger twitched to punch Molly's phone number into her cell and ask her if a God she'd never prayed to would consider her one of His children. She couldn't ask Nick. She'd admitted too much.

Steph let the conversation lag as he headed toward the house. She needed to stop asking questions about things she didn't understand. She beckoned him inside. "I need to let Fred out. He's been home all day."

She walked ahead, then paused and looked over her shoulder as Fred danced around Nick's feet with no eagerness to go outside. She couldn't help but smile. "That's what I call abandonment. He likes you best."

"No one would choose me over you." He patted his leg. "Follow me, pal."

Fred's toenails tapped on the hardwood floor as he followed Nick to the patio doorway.

Steph stepped onto the flagstones, and Nick followed with Fred at his side, but it was too late: she spotted Martin in the yard with Suzette. Before she could stop him, Fred bolted onto the grass and beelined toward the fence.

"Fred, come." She clapped her hands.

The dog skidded to a halt, faltering a moment before he trotted back.

Steph watched Martin as he vanished inside with Suzette. She pressed her hand against her chest, grateful she'd avoided another confrontation. What was it with Martin?

Nick hadn't seemed to notice since he'd been focused on Fred. "He amazes me. He minds every time you call." He swung around to face her.

"He'd better. He's had obedience training." Each time Fred did as she commanded, she remembered

Molly's insistence that she learn how to train the dogs. "After I finished my classes, Fred was my first student. You've seen how he obeys." She captured the dog's attention. "Sit."

Fred sat.

Nick stood beside her and planted his fists on his hips. "Too bad you can't train my brother."

Steph blinked, wondering if Nick had noticed him after all. "Your brother doesn't listen. Believe me."

"But I do." He squeezed her arm. "You look very nice." He stepped back and eyed her again. "It's the color. Your eyes are beautiful."

She gazed down at her cornflower-blue pants with a coordinating knit top and her casual T-strap shoes. Heat swept to her cheeks. "Thank you."

"Like a summer sky."

If she'd struggled with her pulse before, today she'd lost the battle, and her voice found its freedom. "You look good, too. Handsome."

Fred didn't like being ignored, and he tripped Nick trying to get his attention.

Steph grasped Nick's arm. "Fred. No."

The dog backed up and waited.

Nick chuckled. "Fred needs attention. Can I try some of that obedience stuff?"

"Why not? You've watched me." His eagerness and love for dogs seemed to parallel hers.

Nick stepped away with Fred jigging around

his feet, and Steph realized she needed the treats. She held up her index finger and darted into the house, grabbed a few dog food nuggets from the bag and returned to Nick, who looked at her as if she'd lost her mind.

"Dogs need rewards." She beckoned him back, then dropped a few pellets into his hand. "You have to sound commanding. Use a single word— come, sit, stay, down—to get to the point, and make sure you have his attention. Give it a try." She patted Nick's back, feeling the hard muscle beneath her palm, and she had to stop herself from letting her hand linger there. "Ready?" She held Fred's collar.

"As I'll ever be."

Her stomach tightened, watching Nick amble toward the back of the yard. He seemed to be everything a woman would want. She wrapped her arms around herself, imagining they were Nick's. He'd often given her a friendly hug, but an embrace would be a taste of affection that might make her feel whole again.

Nick turned to face her, and Steph released Fred's collar. "Fred, come."

Fred's ears perked. He tilted his head, then bounded to his side.

Nick's head jerked back. "Good boy, Fred." He opened his hand and gave him a treat.

The dog stood in front of him, wagging his tail.

"Sit." He pointed to the ground. "Stay." A grin grew on his mouth as he strode back across the lawn to Steph.

She looked at Fred waiting as he'd been told, his tail smacking the grass.

Nick gave her a wink, then faced Fred. "Come."

The dog trotted across the grass to Nick's side and he tossed him a nugget.

Steph settled into a chair on the patio and watched him play with Fred. She'd fought the battle between head and heart since she'd met Nick, and watching him, she battled with her senses again. People could just be friends. Enjoying Nick's company didn't have to be a romance. But her unsettling sensations when they were together had become too common. If she could control the emotions that changed friendship to something deeper, she might have a lasting relationship with him. She wanted to follow his lead, to accept their relationship for what it was and let it end there.

Maybe, just maybe, they could talk about it. Really talk. He needed to know where she stood, and maybe if she confessed how he rattled her emotions, he'd stop. But she'd be devastated if he looked at her as if she were crazy, and said, "Who said this was anything but friendship?" She couldn't take that.

Something bothered Nick. She'd seen it in his eyes even before they'd discussed her lack of faith, and it troubled her that as great as he was he lived beneath his brother's control. If Martin moved a finger, Nick filled his wishes. It wasn't good for either of them, but then how could she—

"I'm serious, Steph."

She raised her head as her thoughts flittered away.

"Suzette could use training like this. A lot of training. Martin lets her get away with too much."

Steph drew up her shoulders. "I'm sure she would do well." She paused, hating to disappoint him. "But the owner has to learn to work with the dog, too."

A glint flashed in his eyes. "How about the owner's brother?"

Her heart gave a kick, and she wanted to scream. So much for controlling her emotions. "You're with Suzette more than Martin, and maybe he'll take some tips from you." A smile broke through her emotional frustration. "I'm happy to bring Molly some business."

He gave her a thoughtful look. "But I'd like you as the trainer."

She should have guessed. A warm sensation rolled to her chest. More time with Nick. More internal struggle.

"Why not?" she said, knowing they needed to have a serious talk.

* * *

Nick jumped Steph's fence and entered Martin's house through the back door. He opened the refrigerator, grabbed a soda and popped it open, then leaned against the counter. He liked Steph too much. He'd hoped to remain friends, but his heart hadn't kept up with his plan. It had bounded on its merry way, leaving him unprotected from more hurt.

Though upsetting, her confession the other day hadn't surprised him. She'd never said a word about her faith, and though someone could believe without talking about it, he noticed her tension when he mentioned his beliefs or talked about what God would want him to do.

Now he thought more seriously on the topic. What kind of future would they have? He didn't know if he should step away and avoid carving another wound in his heart or hope that something wonderful could happen. He'd said it today when she mentioned holding the Bible in her lap. Why had it been there? If curiosity drew her to the Word, the action could be God's leading. Uncertainty swayed in his mind. One day they needed to talk— really talk—about values and beliefs important to both of them.

Her image clung to his thoughts, and each day he'd watched his admiration grow. Her kindness to his mother overwhelmed him. He couldn't picture

Cara doing that. But Steph did and without being asked. Men weren't supposed to be weak. He'd never admitted his difficulty dealing with emotions to anyone except Steph. She'd listened and didn't back away from being honest that she didn't understand.

Neither did he, but since talking to her and to himself, he'd asked God to forgive him, and now he hoped to make up for his negligence. He'd visited his mom twice in the past few days. She'd been thrilled with the flowers, and he'd noticed improvement in her condition. Steph had said it would happen, and she'd been right.

Steph. He couldn't stop thinking about her. For so long he avoided dating, even considering another relationship. He'd believed it was the right thing to do, but he sensed the Lord had other plans. Whether Steph or someone else, he realized that love of a man and woman was part of God's plan. The proof was in Genesis.

Remaining friends with Steph might have worked, but he'd let his guard down, and now he'd fallen for her. In a big way. Something about her told him she wouldn't walk out on him if they made a commitment. Steph had too much strength. On the day of the fiasco with Martin, she hadn't backed down from his brother as many people did. Nick liked that quality. She'd looked determined and spirited, ready for battle. Nick wished he could be that confident.

Martin, on the other hand, looked confident, but his I'm-always-right attitude lacked Steph's conviction. Martin came off as bullying, and bullies were often cowards. Could it be possible that Martin actually lacked confidence, and his arrogant attitude was a cover? That would make sense. But how could that have happened?

Nick stood a moment, organizing his thoughts. He wanted to understand Martin, and even more he wanted to understand himself. Were the two questions connected?

With his head empty of answers, he drew up his shoulders, then lowered them as he marched into the living room.

Martin sat in a recliner, clutching the phone against his ear. He gave Nick a quick glance, then returned his attention to the telephone call. "Deal with it. I'll be there tomorrow, Reg. I can't solve every problem. That's why I have you."

Nick strolled to the sofa and stretched out, his ear half tuned in to the conversation while his thoughts clung to Steph. The slam of the receiver jarred his reverie. He swung his feet over the edge of the cushion and sat up. "What's the problem?"

Martin drew in a lengthy breath and released it in a huff. "Work details. I've hired idiots."

Nick had heard that before, and he knew what was coming next.

The recliner footrest dropped as Martin straightened. "That's why I wish you'd give up your little business and work for me. I need someone with a brain." He pressed his hands against the chair arm and rose.

"Thanks for acknowledging I have one." The plea was an old one Nick had heard since he'd left Martin's employ and had gone into business for himself. "But is it necessary to belittle my company, Martin? Give it a chance. No one starts a new company on top. They're small before they grow."

His brother swung around to face him. "Why not stay at the top?"

Nick ran his fingers through his hair. "I don't want to work for you. I'm happy being my own boss. There's nothing else to say."

Though Martin's mouth opened as if to continue, he closed it, and silence fell between them.

Counting the seconds, Nick waited until he couldn't keep still. "For an intelligent man, you either speak or act before you think. You don't give me credit for having enough intelligence to run my own business, and you've created hard feelings with your neighbor…and a woman to boot."

"What's the difference?" He shook his head. "Forget it. I don't want to argue with you, too." Martin tossed his cell phone onto the lamp table.

Nick leaned back against the cushion, his mind

whirring. "I don't want to argue with you, either. It seems as if you'd want to try and be neighborly to whoever lives there. It makes life easier."

Martin snorted. "For you."

For you? The comment meant something, but Nick was at a loss.

"Don't give me that deer-in-the-headlights look. I saw you there today, coming out of her house with her and that mutt. What's going on between you two?"

The question knocked the wind out of Nick. He'd wanted to have a serious talk with Martin about his feelings and hoped to get to the bottom of his confusion.

Martin tossed his hands in the air. "I realized she meant more to you than her dog, but I'm not going to jeopardize Suzette for any reason if that's what you're trying to do."

"We're friends. I admire her, and I'm not doing anything that involves Suzette." He felt heat rise up his neck and his blood pressure soar. "In fact, dear brother, I spend more time with your dog than you do. Do you realize that?"

Martin rolled his eyes.

"Who runs over here every time you work late or have a business dinner—which is often. Who takes her for walks?" Nick rose and slapped his chest. "Who jumps at your beck and call? And by the way, Suzette needs obedience training. I'm sure you won't have time for that, either."

A smirk rose on Martin's face. "So that's it."

Nick drew back. "What does that mean?"

"She's twisted you around her finger, and now she's getting even by telling you not to give me the time of day." His eyes blazed. "I thought you'd given up on women. You're still moping over Cara."

"Keep Cara out of this. It has nothing to do with Steph." Fire burned in his gut. "This has nothing to do with either of them anyway. It has to do with how you treat people." Martin's accusation rang in Nick's ears. He wasn't moping over Cara. He was wounded by her attack. But why had he clung to it?

"Here's how I feel." Martin thrust his index finger at Nick. "This is my home, and I don't want that mongrel messing with Suzette."

Nick caved into his chair and threw himself against the cushion. "Martin, Suzette is a dog."

"An expensive one." He shook his head and sent Nick a piercing gaze.

"What's the difference? Fred won't hurt her."

"You don't get it. I paid mucho bucks for a purebred from a good line. I plan to breed her."

Nick felt his eyebrows arch to his hairline. "You're kidding. I thought you wanted a companion." Companion? Suzette had become his companion.

"She is, but I can still breed her. What would I do if she had a litter of mixed puppies?"

Nick gritted his teeth. "Fred's neutered."

"It's a matter of principle."

Nick straightened his back, his head spinning with revelations he needed to deal with. He'd wanted to ask Martin's opinion. What made them tick and— Forget it. He'd accomplished nothing today.

"This is a matter of my principle, Martin. The next time you need someone to go for your laundry or babysit Suzette, you'd better find someone other than me."

Nick rose and marched to the door.

Chapter Six

When Steph turned down her street, an older car was parked in front of her house—one she didn't recognize. When she passed it, Steph spotted a man inside. Her stomach tightened. Hal. His dishwater blond hair hung over his ears as he slouched in his seat. She released a lengthy breath, irked that he'd come without calling.

She supposed he'd warned her with his "I'll see you soon" as she'd hung up. That had been two weeks earlier. Now here he was. Steph pulled into the driveway, steadied herself and slipped outside.

A thud resounded as Hal slammed his car door and bounded toward her, his long arms open, his lanky body and pale skin making him look as if he'd never seen the sun. "Steph. I'm here."

She managed to step into his embrace, then back

away and studied his face, wishing she had a warmer welcome. "How are you?"

He drew back, still holding her shoulders. "You don't seem very pleased to see me."

"I'm surprised. I expected you to call first."

He lengthened his six-foot frame. "I did. Don't you remember?"

"I know you called a couple weeks ago, but—" she waved her hand in the air, forcing her lungs to draw in a full breath "—I'm involved in a wedding this weekend so it's not a great time to entertain."

He slipped his arm around her shoulder—a warning sign he needed something—and gave her a one-armed hug. "No need to entertain. I can make myself at home."

That's what she feared. "How's Dad?"

"Gnarly as ever." He dropped his arm and opened the storm door while she slid her key into the lock. "I'll need one of those."

Her brows knit together. "One of what?" She knew very well what he wanted.

"The key. I can't make myself at home without a key."

She lowered her head rather than make another less-than-pleasant comment.

As soon as his feet hit the foyer, Fred trotted to his side and sniffed his pant leg.

"Scram, buster."

Too much for Steph, she drew up her shoulders. "It's Fred, and please say 'no.' He understands what that means." Turning her back on the two of them, she set her tracks for the patio door to let Fred outside; but before she did, Steph had learned to check Martin's yard. Empty.

That action made her feel resentful, too. Since Martin's tirade, she'd been guarded about letting Fred outside, and she wanted it to stop. Why did she live in fear of another confrontation with him? Because of Nick, she assumed. That put him in the middle. She didn't want to do that.

She pulled the door open to let Fred outside. When a new dog came for the first day, she liked to leave Fred home. Though he was welcoming to other dogs, jealousy came into play when she gave the new one added attention.

Hal stepped outside and scanned the yard. "Looks the same."

She eyed her flowers that bordered the fence, her neat lawn and the shade trees. What did he expect? She slid open the door, rolling her eyes, and stepped into the kitchen with Hal on her heels.

"What's for dinner? I'm starving." He charged past the oak table and tugged open the refrigerator door, then nosed inside.

"Sorry, Hal. I'm leaving for a while. I'll grab something when I'm out." She stopped herself from closing the door on his head. As quickly as her frustration came so did remorse. He may have changed. Maybe her dad had become gnarly. "I need to do some grocery shopping. You might find some eggs and cheese in the meat keeper."

He closed the refrigerator and peered at her. "You want me to cook?"

Her remorse faded. Typical Hal. She shrugged. "Then eat out. There's Franco's up the road in a strip mall. Great Italian. Or try Zoup! Wonderful sandwiches and soup. Just south of Wattles, or you probably passed the Ram's Horn."

He didn't look happy, but then neither did she.

Fred barked outside the patio door, and she slid it open. He bounded in and headed for Hal again. Hal opened his mouth, then thought better and wrapped his tongue around no. Fred skidded to a halt.

Steph grabbed her purse, then halted and opened a drawer. "Here's an extra key to the front. Make sure you lock up when you go." She took another step, then stopped again. "And keep Fred inside. I have a cranky neighbor."

Hal gave her a quick nod. "Fine."

"I'll see you later." She left the kitchen, then rolled her shoulders backward to relax them. Nick's talk about how God wanted Christians to behave came back to haunt her. Her action and attitude weren't charitable, and she knew treating er brother badly wasn't godly. She slipped into her car and pulled away, struggling with the emotion—negative emotion based on nothing but he past. People could change. She'd worked hrough problems in her life, and she'd changed or the better. She certainly hadn't transformed to glory as the Bible verses had talked about when he read to Julia, but she'd become more outgoing again and more confident. At least most of he time.

Julia. Guilt spiraled through her. She'd thought about visiting Julia today, and now Hal had motivated her to act on her thought. Part of her wanted to put her feet up and relax. She'd eat cereal or an egg and toast. The last thing she wanted to do was cook a meal.

The rehabilitation center sign appeared ahead, nd Steph moved into the right lane, then into to he parking lot. Nick said Julia had made progress, nd she'd neglected to go back even though she'd planned to. Julia would want her to read the Bible. She knew it, but she didn't think that was what kept er from returning. In fact, the Bible had made her urious, and she wanted to know why.

She headed inside and made her way to Julia's room. At the doorway, she paused in case she was asleep, but Julia turned her head and gave her crooked smile. Steph entered the room and stood beside her bed. "You look chipper today How are you?"

"Bettah."

"Better. That's great." She looked around th room and noticed a walker. "Are you getting up?"

Her shoulder lifted in a faint shrug. "Little."

"A little is better than being in bed all the time."

"Yes." Julia grinned.

Steph shifted to the chair she'd occupied the firs time she came and sat. Another bouquet ha replaced the other. She couldn't see the card, an the books she'd purchased were still on the table So was the Bible.

Thinking of things to talk about with someon she barely knew caused her to falter. What topic were appropriate? She couldn't tell her about he faith issues or her struggle not to fall in love wit Nick. There was always Fred. She paused. Ha hardly seemed like an appropriate topic. She reall didn't want to talk about him. She leaned back an released a sigh.

Julia noticed. "Okay?" She pointed to her.

Uncomfortable that she'd been so obvious, Step leaned forward, managed a smile and changed he mind. "I'm fine. Just a busy day. I have the doggi day care, and when I arrived home, my brother wa waiting for me. He came for a visit."

Julia nodded. "Nice."

The word was much clearer today, sending a natural smile to Steph's face. "I'm so glad to hear you talking so much better. I know you'll be happier when you can talk again."

"Yes." Her eyes searched Steph's. "Motha?"

Mother. Steph controlled her emotions. "My mom died a couple years ago. Her heart. Very quickly."

"Oh. Sorry."

"Thank you. She was a wonderful mother." And so was Julia. She could tell. Steph would have been more relaxed, helping her with therapy, maybe walking in the corridor, but she suspected Julia wasn't ready for that yet. She eyed the novels, but her focus settled on the Bible. "Would you like me to read to you?"

Julia's eyes brightened.

Steph wanted to grasp one of the novels, but she knew what she had to do. She lay her hand on the Bible. "This?"

Julia's smile answered her question.

This time she opened the pages at the bookmark. She scanned the page, realizing someone else must have read to her. Martin or Nick? "Did someone read to you?"

"Nick."

Her heart jumped, hearing his name. "I'll start at 2 Corinthians chapter four. Is that good?"

"Good." Julia rolled on to her back and used her left hand to bring her right one to her chest.

Steph began the chapter, hearing again the message of the blinded minds of nonbelievers and the veil that kept them from seeing the truth. She read the words, but her mind tried to dissect the meaning. She wanted to understand. God shed light into hearts and took them out of darkness. Was that the emptiness and loneliness she'd felt for so long?

Once again, Nick's face hung in her mind, glowing with the faith so important to him. She wanted that glow, but it seemed hopeless.

Steph finished verse fifteen and began the last verses of that chapter. "Therefore we do not lose heart. Though outwardly we are wasting away, yet inwardly we are being renewed day by day. For our light and momentary troubles are achieving for us an eternal glory that far outweighs them all. So we fix our eyes not on what is seen, but on what is unseen. For what is seen is temporary, but what is unseen is eternal."

Her heart leaped with the message, words she struggled to understand, but sensed that she did. *So we fix our eyes not on what is seen, but on what is unseen. For what is seen is temporary, but what is unseen is eternal.* She wished she could talk with Nick's mother, because Julia could help her understand the concept.

Moisture rimmed her eyes, and she lifted her finger and wiped it away, hoping Julia didn't notice. Frustration anchored her to the chair. How could she ask Nick's mother when she couldn't answer?

When she lifted her eyes, Julia looked at her with question.

Instead of talking, she reread the last verses again, then lifted her head. "What is unseen?"

Julia's eyebrows lifted, then lowered as if she didn't understand.

"Does this mean people pay attention to the world and everything we can see, but they should be looking at things they can't see?"

Julia patted her left hand on the bed. "Come."

Steph rose and sat beside her, wanting to touch her hand, to feel the comfort that her mother had given her when she was a frightened child.

"God."

"The unseen is God?" She should have known. "God is eternal."

Julia rested her palm on Steph's hand. "You. Me."

"Eternal." Her pulse fluttered. "We are eternal with God."

Julia lifted her finger and pointed upward. "Heaven."

"In heaven." Steph couldn't speak with her mind flying in so many directions. She'd envisioned herself vanishing from the earth. Becoming dirt that fertilized the soil. Nothing more.

Julia's hand pressed hers, and a sense of well-being rolled through Steph like a breeze that ruffled her hair or kissed her cheek. She couldn't see it, but she knew it was there.

Nick swung around the doorway, then darted back. His heart rose to his throat—Steph and his mom talking about God. About God? He'd prayed and hoped, but so soon? The scene amazed him. He stayed out of sight, listening to Steph's questions and his mother's one- or two-word responses. He wanted to walk in and answer her questions, explain what he believed, but he couldn't. He'd listened but shouldn't have without her knowledge.

When the questions died, he stepped away, then turned and headed back, making as much noise as he could to alert them. When he rounded into the room, his mother smiled, and Steph looked over her shoulder, then rose. Her cheeks flushed as he approached.

"Steph. This is nice." He carried the bouquet of flowers to his mother and bent to kiss her. "For you."

"Beautiful."

He turned to Steph. "Listen to that. She said every letter. Mom's having problems with *R*s. That's it." He gave his mother's hand a pat and set the flowers on the windowsill, then scrutinized the other flowers. "These are still looking pretty good."

Nick felt like a voyeur trying to hide his guilt. He wanted to lead the conversation back to the Bible, but he knew it was better to let it drop. "I'd planned to drop by after dinner. I'll bring those stones over tomorrow so we can get your rock garden set up."

"Thanks." She eyed him a moment. "Guess who arrived today."

"Who arrived?" She didn't look happy about it. He thought a moment. "Your brother?"

She nodded. "He wasn't happy that I didn't cook dinner."

That made him smile. "I'm glad he came. When I bring those rocks, he can help me get them into the backyard."

She gave him a doubtful grin. "You think so?"

"You don't think he'd help if I asked?"

This time she laughed. "I can't wait until tomorrow."

"Hal, that's where I found you last night when I got back." Steph struggled not to jam her fists on her hips. "Could you turn down the TV?"

Her brother shifted and grabbed the TV remote from beneath him as he lay sprawled on the sofa. He smacked the remote and lowered the volume, then arched an eyebrow at her. "What got you in a huff?"

If she were honest, she'd tell him, but she wanted to follow Nick's philosophy—God's, really—to be kind and compassionate. The job was taxing. "We have a lot of things to do tonight."

"We?" He shifted the sofa pillow beneath his head, his gaze drifting to a sports show.

"Nick should be here any minute, and he'll need help moving some rocks to the backyard."

"Rocks? This isn't prison camp, is it?"

Steph bit her tongue to control her comment. "I hoped you'd be willing to help him."

"I have a bad back." He gave a grimace as he rolled to his side. "I'd hurt it again."

Steph had never heard about the bad back before, but it figured. He'd spent time laying on the sofa since he'd arrived. "Is this why Dad and you had problems?" She motioned to his reclined position.

His attention had drifted back to the TV so her gesture and comment had been lost.

"When's dinner?"

"After we do the rocks." She marched into the kitchen, checked Martin's yard, then let Fred outside.

Eyeing the wall clock, she glanced at her watch. Nick had said he'd be there when she got home at six. She'd gotten hung up at the shelter, and now it was six-thirty. Instead of wasting time, she made a salad, her eyes drifting to the clock hands. Picking up the rocks had been Nick's idea, a favor to her, so she couldn't be angry, but she'd noticed lateness seemed to be part of his character.

She scrubbed three potatoes, pricked them with a fork and set them in the microwave. Then all she needed to do was punch the button. The clock read seven-fifteen. Her stomach growled. They could eat first, but doing heavy work after eating didn't strike her as a relaxing dinner.

Hal appeared at her side, eyeing her preparations. "I thought you were making dinner."

"After the rocks." She dropped the pork chops into a marinade and shook her head.

"Where is the dude?"

That's what she wanted to know. Although she felt nervy, Steph grabbed her purse and pulled out her cell, then pressed Nick's number. Hal hovered nearby with his head in the refrigerator while she waited. His voice mail clicked in. Her shoulder's tensed. What was wrong?

"You need to go grocery shopping." Hal's lanky frame hung on the door like a whiny teenager.

"How about you picking up some groceries? Get what you like. The stove's sitting here all day long." Her sarcasm was tinged with some regret. Her patience had "flown the coop" as her mother used to say.

"I'm a little short on cash. Can you loan me a few bucks?"

She drew in a deep stream of breath and released it. "Hal, you need to get this straight. Doug made a good salary, but he's not here to bail you out. I had money back then. I don't anymore. You need to fend for yourself. Dad and I can't do it anymore."

"I didn't say give me money. I said loan."

A laugh burst from her, verging on hysteria. Her hands knotted into fists and a nerve ticked in her cheek. "You still owe me thousands for loans, Hal. I'm telling you I don't have it."

He swaggered to a counter and rested his back against it. "So you're telling me Doug left you destitute?"

The smirk on his face chilled her to the bone. "I haven't told this to anyone, but I'm going to tell you. Doug left me in debt except for the house. He'd lost tons of money gambling. I had no idea. He took care of the bills." Tears inched to her eyes, tears she'd thought ended long ago.

Hal jammed his hands into his pockets. "Come on. You guys were loaded. He couldn't have—"

She flexed her palm upward like a cop. "He did. I was nearly broke." She brushed the tears with the back of her hand, wanting to scream. Three years she struggled to pull her life together. She had no skills for working and no confidence. Being an executive's wife meant socializing and entertaining. That's all she'd done. "I told you to get a job and make up with Dad until you can get your own place, but you didn't listen."

"That's what I plan to do, but not with Dad. I came here."

She drew back with such force, she whacked her head against the edge of a cabinet door. "You're kidding. You think you can stay with me while you look for work. Michigan is in bad shape. People are out of work all over the place. The auto industry is laying off, not hiring. You're not making sense."

"Thanks. I thought you'd understand. I am your brother." He dug his hand into a bag of cookies and stomped as best he could with stockings out of the kitchen.

If she weren't so upset, she might have laughed. Instead gooseflesh prickled down her arms. Dealing with Hal seemed to be more than she could handle today. And Nick? She eyed the clock— nearly eight. Something must have happened. God, if you're really there… What was she doing? If there was a God, He'd be irked at her prayer while questioning His existence, and if He wasn't there, her prayer was useless.

But lately she'd begun to sense—

"Someone's here."

Hal's shout broke her thought. She headed to the door, and as soon as she entered the living room, she saw Nick through the window and her pulse accelerated. He was okay.

She stood at the door, and he stepped in. "Sorry I'm late. I ran into some snags."

"You didn't call." She wanted to say so much more.

"I left my cell phone at work. I'm really sorry." He glanced at Hal spread out on the sofa, giving him the eye.

"Tell that to my stomach." Hal didn't lift his head.

"Hal." Steph narrowed her eyes. "This is Nick." She turned to him, arching a brow. "My brother, Hal."

Hal managed to pull himself up from his reclined position and grasped Nick's offered hand.

Nick gave it a shake but kept his eyes on Steph. "I held up your dinner. I'm really sorry."

"I thought we'd move the stones first, then eat."

He nodded. "I know, but…" He hitched his shoulder toward Hal.

She gave a quick shake of her head, hoping he would let it drop.

He shrugged and turned to her brother. "Could you help me carry some rocks into the back?"

Hal shifted, adding his infamous grimace. "Sorry, man, I have a bad back."

Nick flashed Steph a helpless expression as she sent him a told-you-so look. "I'll help you."

"It's a man's job, Steph. You're a woman." He

glanced over his shoulder at her brother, then dropped his arms to his sides when he saw no reaction.

"I'm glad you noticed" slipped through her mind, but lighthearted comments didn't fit the tension she felt.

"I'll get some work gloves and meet you out front."

His frustration evident, Nick headed for the front door as Steph turned away.

Steph stepped into the garage, a place that still held horrible memories. She grabbed the gloves from a bench near the door, slipped them on her hands and hurried back into the fresh air. Fred followed at her feet, and Steph sent him back into the house so he wouldn't escape with the gate open, then headed around the front, her spirit weighted with concerns about Hal and Nick.

She liked Nick so much, but at times he seemed thoughtless. His lateness and not calling ahead of time. Yet he was thoughtful in so many other ways. Today stood out as an example. He had an excuse today, but she'd been worried about his safety. Serious accidents happen without warning.

She remembered Doug's death, and maybe that's why she'd become so sensitive.

On the way to the front, she passed Nick carrying a stone. He grinned, but it looked more like a scowl with the weight he carried. She reached the SUV and searched for a rock she could lift. Hal's help would have been appreciated, and she could have worked on dinner. The idea ruffled her. She tugged off the gloves and marched into the house.

The sofa was empty, and she hurried down the hallway to the guest room. No Hal. When she returned to the living room, she noticed his car was gone. She slammed her hand against the storm door handle and marched back outside through the garage. She had to have something there to make moving the stones easier, even a dolly.

Nick came through the gate and stopped. He set the rock on the driveway, pulled off his gloves and shoved them into his back pocket, then headed toward her.

"Hal's gone."

He nodded. "He left right after I came out to the car." He rubbed his hands against his pants. "I suppose he was afraid you'd insist he help."

She massaged the back of her neck. "That's what I'd planned to do." She shook her head. "I wish I had a wheelbarrow."

He shrugged. "Let me get these. You go in and start dinner."

When she protested, he grasped her by the shoulders and marched her toward the door. She expected him to head back out, but instead, he turned her around to face him. His eyes searched hers.

"You don't deserve being treated like that,

Steph." He pressed his palm against her cheek. "I know you think I'm doing too much for Martin, and you're right. I am, but—"

"I'm doing the same with Hal."

He gave a single nod and didn't move.

The look in his eyes tingled through her chest, a tenderness she had only dreamed about.

"You're amazing." His index finger moved against her cheek, then lowered his hand and traced the line of her lips.

Steph's heart swelled and pressed against her lungs. Nick moved in slow motion, his mouth lowering to hers, an urging so gentle, she yielded with no thought to logic or reason. She'd responded from her heart. When he drew back, his face reflected his surprise and his pleasure. His mouth curved to a gentle smile. "I didn't plan that, but it seemed so natural."

She couldn't speak but let her eyes answer him. He drew her close and held her against his chest as if she belonged there.

He used his cheek to brush her hair from her ear, then whispered, "We could stay here all day, but it won't build you a rock garden."

His breath tickled her, and she drew back. "Or cook your dinner."

He chuckled, and as they parted, the first sense of uneasiness marred the warm feeling she'd experienced. He squeezed her hand, then slipped on his gloves and headed out of the garage.

Steph caught her breath and made her way to the kitchen. All she could do was lean against the counter and relive the moment. How had it happened? She tried to remember what had been said. Had she given him a look? She rubbed her temples. Stop. It just happened. And she loved it. But why in the garage?

Fred leaned against her leg, and when she noticed his plaintive look, she laughed. Steph gave him some food to get him away from her feet, then washed her hands in the sink, imagining the idiotic smile she had on her face.

Trying to focus on dinner, Steph pulled the pork chops from the refrigerator. Though she'd preferred to grill them, time didn't allow it, and then she'd have to be outside and face Nick again. The more reality settled in the more confused she became.

She paused a moment, clutching the package of chops, returning to their conversation before the kiss. Brothers. Hal and Martin. Different men but the same problem. The revelation put a damper on her thoughts.

Instead of grilling, Steph poured a splash of oil in a frying pan, browned the meat, then added a can of mushroom soup and covered the skillet. The chops were always tender that way.

To give herself more time to get her emotions in check, she set the kitchen table, not a romantic dining room meal. Confident Hal would be back, she laid three place settings. His instinct seemed to alert him when dinner was ready.

Taking a deep breath, Steph slid open the door and stepped outside. From the patio, Steph watched Nick hoist the rocks and maneuver them into place.

She wandered closer, noticing two large bags of soil to make the garden. He thought of everything. "How's it going?"

Nick tilted his head toward her. Perspiration beaded on his forehead. He straightened and gave her a grin as he swung his arm toward the stones. "What do you think?"

She gazed at the rock formation he'd constructed. "I like it. It's functional, and it'll be really pretty with flowers. I'd like to do that in a couple more spots."

He pressed his hands against his waist and leaned back, stretching his muscles. "How many?"

She laughed at his expression, and it felt amazing. Laughter had faded from her life since Hal arrived, and she shouldn't have let it. "It can wait."

He reached for her with his soiled gloves, and she ducked from his grasp. "Dinner will be ready in twenty minutes or so."

"I'll be finished." He stood aside, eyeing the stones, then used a pocketknife to slit open one of the sacks of dirt. "I'll add the dirt, then I'll be finished." He looked over and gave her a wink. "The flowers are your job."

The wink floated through her chest. "That's the fun part." She managed a grin, then paused a moment before she spoke. "I had a revelation when I was inside."

He arched his eyebrow, but a playful look lit his eyes. "A revelation. This could be interesting."

She hoped he didn't misunderstand what she was going to say. "You and I really do have the same problem."

His grin yielded to a frown. "Which one?"

That made her chuckle. "Our brothers, as we said earlier."

"Ah. Yes. We both have them, and they are problems." He slit open the next bag.

She stepped closer. "You know, Nick, the problem is ours. We let them run over us." She ran her hand down her pant leg. "Hal assumes I'm going to bow to his wishes. Today he asked me for a loan."

Nick let the bag slip to the ground and straightened.

"I don't have money to loan, Nick. I struggle sometimes to pay my bills. The new facility has helped, and I have more dogs now, but it's been hard."

He studied her face, compassion flooding his eyes. It was the last thing she wanted to see.

"I'm not asking for pity. I can manage, but I'm far from rich like your brother or you."

His expression changed to surprise. "You have it wrong. I'm not rich. Do you think I'd live in an apartment if I could afford a house?"

Apartment. She'd forgotten. "They're easier. No yard work or outside maintenance." She shook her head. "But if you own a business, I assumed—"

"It's a young company, Steph. It'll be great in a few years, I hope, but now I'm careful how I spend money." He held up his hand to keep her from talking. "But that's not the point. If your brother's not helping himself, then your help is enabling."

"You do that with Martin. Not with money but with your time and energy." She expected him to get defensive, but he didn't. He only nodded.

"I told him the other day he needs to find someone else to run his errands."

The news caught her off-guard. "What did he say?"

"Nothing. I walked out of the house."

Her chest tightened as she pictured Nick turning his back on Martin and strutting from the house. "Really?"

His face grew serious. "Really. I haven't talked to him since that day. I think he knew I meant it."

He stepped closer, pulled off his gloves and drew her to him. "It's difficult, but maybe that's what you need to do with Hal."

She thought of him when he was a little boy—so cute; she'd adored him. He'd been indulged, and he would never learn if she continued to let him get away with it. "You're right, but it isn't easy."

"He needs a job. That's what he needs."

He cupped her head with his hand, his eyes riveted to hers—his so close.

Steph's pulse skipped, wondering if he was about to kiss her again.

"I see I haven't missed dinner."

Hal's voice jerked them apart.

She looked at Nick, his eyes questioning as her mind filled with her own questions. She drew back, her anxious heart quieting. "Wash up, and we'll eat."

Nick didn't comment. He turned and headed for the house.

Chapter Seven

When Nick closed his car door, he heard Suzette in the backyard. He ambled back, hoping Fred and Steph were out. Instead, the dog sat beneath a tree, yipping at a red squirrel sitting above her in the branches. It looked like a face-off. He grinned, thinking of Fred's squirrel attack.

Hal's car still sat in front of Steph's, and though he wanted to talk with him about a job idea, he leaned against the fence, hoping to see Steph. So much had changed with the kiss. He'd wanted to kiss her for the past two weeks, but wisdom stopped him. He hadn't felt ready for romance, and then she hadn't been a Christian. But seeing her read the Bible, asking his mother questions about God's meaning in the verses, all these things gave him hope and his concern had subsided.

Still, kissing her two days ago had startled him.

It had happened as naturally as the sun going down in the evening and had been as beautiful. Her amazing smile, her full lips that looked soft—and they were—never left his mind. For a man who'd crossed women off his list for so long, his action didn't fit his plan, and today his enthusiasm to see her didn't fit, either. He sensed his plan slipping away. His feelings were real. Now to resolve the pile of problems that insisted on ruining his life. He planned to start now.

Today, he would apologize to Martin. If his mother learned about their tiff, it would be one more situation that would add to her unhappiness. He and Martin needed to stick together, at least for his mother's sake. Anyway he knew that repentance and forgiveness went hand in hand, so he wanted to tell Martin he was sorry for his behavior. He still didn't plan to be Martin's gofer.

Then came Hal. Nick had witnessed Steph's stress with her brother. During dinner, Hal had made a few snide remarks about Nick's lateness. Nick regretted that, and he observed Steph's uneasiness with Hal's comment. But she babied her brother and couldn't seem to stop.

Still, breaking old habits took time. He'd mentioned the problem of enabling, and she seemed to understand, but acting on it took more courage than talking. He knew that from his own relation-ship with Martin.

From their conversation at dinner, Nick sensed the problem could get worse. Hal made the point that he planned to stay in Michigan and look for work. He obviously assumed he'd stay with Steph.

Nick had no thought of resolving all his issues in one day, but he and Steph needed to talk about them. And they needed to talk about their relation-ship. Until their kiss when he showed Steph affec-tion, reticence appeared in her eyes. But her actions didn't match the look. She seemed to have enjoyed his romantic advances. Who was he to question? He'd acted the same way.

Nick cut short his thoughts when he noticed Steph's new rock garden. She'd already planted flowers, colorful ones that would weave around the stones. He smiled, picturing her on her knees, probably fighting off Fred, to place the flowers in the perfect spot.

The patio door slid open, jarring Nick's pulse, but instead of Steph, Hal stepped out along with Fred, who bounded to greet Suzette. Hal gave him a suspicious look while he strolled across the grass.

Nick raised his hand in greeting.

"She's not home." Hal faced him across the fence.

"You mean, Steph?"

"Who else?"

His smugness grated, but he shrugged it off. "I wanted to talk with you anyway."

If ever Nick had seen someone's defenses rise, he saw it today. "About what?"

"About a job."

Hal folded his arms across his chest, a sneer growing on his face. "And?"

"I own a company that makes parts for tools."

Hal's eyebrow made a subtle arch.

"I don't have an opening today, but I'll have one in a week or so. If you'd like to drop by the office, I'd be happy to have you fill out an application and talk to you about the job." He pulled out his wallet and extended his business card.

Hal eyed it with disdain. "What's the catch?"

Nick drew back. "Catch? There is none."

His stark gaze softening, Hal's brow lowered. "Is it an office job?"

Office job? He had to be kidding. "No. It's in the factory, but the work isn't heavy so it won't bother your back." Why was he trying to convince him? The guy came across as useless.

Hal finally grasped the card, glanced at it and shoved it in his shirt pocket. "Thanks."

"You're welcome." He dropped his hands and turned toward Martin's house. As he headed inside, he remembered. Steph had the wedding rehearsal. She'd probably be gone all evening.

He turned and walked backward, clapping his hands. "Suzette."

She peered at him, her eyes peeking through her wispy bangs, then turned and trotted away.

So much for obedience.

He strode back to the fence and caught her collar and forced her to follow. He and Martin needed to talk but leaving Suzette outside with Fred would just cause another argument. At the back door, he paused. Maybe he should go to the front and ring the bell. Nick tossed the idea around, then decided to do what he always did. He opened the back door and dodged Suzette as she darted in, then stepped inside. His nerves kicked in, and he took a lengthy breath to ready himself for whatever. He never knew what to expect with Martin.

Hearing the murmur of the television, Nick headed toward the living room, assuming he'd find Martin there. He stopped in the archway, waiting to be acknowledged.

Martin turned his head, eyed him, then turned back to the news.

Nick ambled in, his mind tangled in how to proceed. He sat on the edge of the sofa, waiting for his brother to speak. He didn't so Nick gave in and broke the silence. "I came to apologize."

"I see." He sat as rigid and unmoving as a statue.

"I'm sorry about walking out the other day. I

don't want to argue with you. For Mom's sake, we need to be…on speaking terms." He'd wanted to say friends but that never would be.

"You're the one who walked out. Not me."

"That's right." He sat, nodding his head. Martin stared at the television. Nick dropped against the cushion and folded his hands.

"What do you want, Nick?" Martin finally turned to face him.

"To get along. To be honest. To—"

"Honest?" Martin's brows knitted. "I've always been honest with you."

Nick struggled with what he wanted to say. The topic seemed too complex to put into words. He raised his back from the cushion and rested his palms on his knees. "May I ask you a question?"

"About what?" He eyed Nick a second, then sank back into the chair.

"About us. About who we are and why." Nick's stomach rolled, and he almost wished he hadn't pursued the topic.

Martin's eyes glazed. "We're the Davis brothers."

"I mean, who we are in here?" He tapped his chest. "I don't understand me half the time, and I wonder if we put our thoughts together it might help me to understand myself."

"You're not making sense to me at all, Nick. Ask Mother."

The dig ripped through Nick's civility. "Right. Thanks for the great idea."

"Sorry." Martin lowered his gaze. "I shouldn't have said that."

The unexpected apology soothed Nick's irritation. "Thank you." He rose and wandered toward the window, looking out at the sun glinting off the hood of his car. "I'm serious." He turned to face him. "I always think of you as the son who could do anything. Me? I bungled along, hoping to make Mom and Dad proud, but I don't think I ever did."

"What?" Martin's tone raised a decibel. "You were the baby. You made them laugh. You gave them joy. Whatever you wanted they gave you. I worked hard to be the best I could and never felt it was enough. They expected me to be on top."

Nick drew back his shoulders, hoping to ease the stress he felt. "I never saw that." His mind soared back to years earlier, trying to envision their childhood. "I think you demanded it of yourself."

"That was you, Nick. Mom and Dad allowed you to make mistakes. I never could."

Nick rubbed his forehead, wishing he hadn't started this today. "I made lots of mistakes. I made them with Cara although I never totally understood. She said I neglected her."

"Maybe she needed too much, Nick. Her walking away might have done you a favor."

A favor? The idea startled him. Had she needed too much? Steph asked for so little. He tried to grasp Martin's words. "I saw her breaking our engagement as failure. Mom and Dad loved Cara. I disappointed them." And he'd disappointed himself

"If you think you let them down, think how often I did. They didn't understand my divorce from Denise. And I wanted things that they didn't want for me. It hurt seeing the disappointment in Mom's eyes and the frustration in Dad's."

Nick dug into his memory. He had no recollection of anything he'd just heard. Martin had always been in his parents' favor. "Like what?"

"It's over. Not up for discussion."

His brother's typical response. Nick disliked when Martin snapped the door closed. "No discussion, but one final thought." He pinpointed Martin's gaze. "Are you spending your life still trying to prove yourself? You can't make yourself better, Martin, by putting other people down."

"What are you talking about?"

"You know what I'm talking about."

They sat in silence while Nick tried to sort out what had been said. Had he learned anything new about himself? Maybe. Martin's comment about Cara hung in his mind. *Maybe she needed too much, Nick. She might have done you a favor.* He'd always blamed himself.

Nick rose and gave his brother's shoulder an amiable shake before walking out the door. He had things to think about, and he prayed Martin did, too.

When Steph walked through the door, Julia was sitting in a chair, her pale cheeks showing a pinky hue, her hazel eyes looking almost olive. "You look wonderful." Steph crossed the tile floor and kissed her on the cheek. Her action surprised her more than Julia.

"Thank you." Julia smiled at Steph, her speech much less labored.

"I have to get my hair curled and you were so close, I decided to make a quick stop."

"I'm glad." Julia reached forward with her left hand, and Steph clasped it in hers, then studied her. "Your hair."

Steph recognized it as a question, and she touched her straight style and grinned. "I'm getting it curled. I'm a bridesmaid in my coworker's wedding."

"Wedding. That's nice." She gave Steph's fingers a faint squeeze then let her hand drop to the blanket. "A friend?"

"My friend Molly's wedding. She has a dog shelter, and I help her with that and then run a doggie day care in the same building."

"I love dogs." Her eyes sparkled. "Martin has one."

Martin. Her *R*s were still weak, but she seemed so much better. "I know. Suzette."

Julia nodded, then studied Steph a moment again before she tilted her head and drew her hand to her chest. "You and Nick?"

"Friends."

Something flashed in her eyes—curiosity or disappointment. "Only?"

Steph's pulse skipped. "Only friends…for now." She watched Julia trying to form words and she longed to help her. "Very good friends, though." Her comment riffled along her arms.

"Someday?" Hope brightened Julia's face.

Though she'd known Nick's mother for only a few weeks, the sense of family she had missed for such a long time embraced her as did Julia's tender look. An urge rose to be open with her. "I'm a widow."

"Oh."

Even with the distortion from the stroke, Steph read sadness in her expression, and she shook her head to help Julia understand. "It was a troubled marriage." Troubled. The weight of the past drained her spirit. She'd kept it a secret so long as if she'd used her own hands to kill Doug. She'd spent years convincing herself she'd been innocent.

Julia studied her, and Steph released her anxiety with a lengthy breath and spilled the story of Doug's dismaying suicide and the problems before his death as if it were stagnant water that ended life. When she'd finished, relief covered her and she was surprised that she'd opened up so quickly.

Julia's face filled with compassion, her altered voice speaking an occasional sound of sympathy.

"I don't tell people about this. Not even Nick."

"No?" Her expression asked why.

"I don't want pity, and it's difficult to trust that pity won't be an influence on relationships. Nick is compassionate." She paused to rephrase the comment. "But he doesn't like to deal with emotion."

"You know him well."

Steph grinned at that. She had begun to know Nick, even some nuances of his character. "I'm afraid he'll stick with me, because I need him and not because he cares about me."

Julia shook her head. "I don't think so." Her gaze drifted before she refocused on Steph. "But I understand."

Steph's mind snapped to another truth, and her pulse raced. "I want you to know another thing that has kept me from moving beyond friendship with Nick. I've never been a believer. He knows, but he's had patience with me. Maybe he has hope."

"Hope. Yes. Always." Julia's eyes searched hers. "But the Bible?"

"Yes, I read it to you. Why? Because I was curious."

"Good."

"Scared but curious." Her pulsed accelerated as she leaned closer. "Here's another secret. I bought a Bible for myself, and I've been reading it. I want to have the peace and hope that Nick and Molly have." She touched Julia's unmoving hand. "And you."

"I'm glad."

"I started reading where I left off with you, and it touched me." The memory washed over her sending a knot to her throat. "I read a verse that explained so many things, and it—"

Steph's cell phone played its jingle and she paused to dig it from her purse. She flipped open the phone and eyed the caller before she pressed the phone to her ear. "Hi, Nick."

"I thought I'd stop over to talk about tonight."

"Molly's sister is picking me up, and we're getting dressed at the church. You know, they do photographs and things."

"So I can't drive you?"

She heard the disappointment in his voice. "You could, but it's not necessary."

"How about if I drop by in a couple hours. We can talk then."

Steph clamped her teeth together, sensing his determination. "Okay. I'll see you then."

She disconnected and grinned at Julia, who'd

slipped back into bed while she was on the phone. "Nick."

Julia only nodded while her gaze swept to the bedside table. "Read the verse."

"The verse?" Then she remembered. Steph grasped the Bible and opened it to 2 Corinthians 12:9-10. Her eyes swept over the passages, then she read. "My grace is sufficient for you, for my power is made perfect in weakness. Therefore I will boast all the more gladly about my weaknesses, so that Christ's power may rest on me. That is why, for Christ's sake, I delight in weaknesses, in insults, in hardships, in persecutions, in difficulties. For when I am weak, then I am strong."

Steph lifted her eyes and gazed at Julia. "I never understood why a God wouldn't stop bad things from happening. Why did He allow people to have problems? Why didn't He make all people strong and protect them from hurt?" She closed her eyes a moment, possibilities wavering in her mind. She drew her shoulders upward. "Then we wouldn't need Him, would we?"

Julia didn't speak.

"When we're weak, then we turn to God for strength. We acknowledge Him and He uses His power for us."

"And we praise Him." Julia's eyes closed and opened. "God wants our thanks and praise."

Though her words were labored and her *R*s non-existent, she spoke with assurance that filled Steph's heart. Tears blurred her eyes. "When I'm confused is when I miss my mother so much. I don't know if she was a believer or not, but she was a good mother. I can never replace her, but you have a mother's heart and—"

Julia patted her chest and beckoned her closer.

Steph sat on the edge of her bed, and Julia drew her head onto her breast and patted her hair as her mother had done.

Steph wept.

Steph tossed her purse on the chair near the door. "Can you sit up?"

"Why?" Hal didn't bother to look at her.

She shook her head and strode to the kitchen to get a soft drink. Her mouth was parched while sitting under the dryer at the beauty salon. After she took a long drink, she wandered into the half bath and caught her reflection in the mirror. Curly hair. She eyed the spiraled waves that looked so different from her straight hair, but she thought curls would be special for Molly's wedding.

She ambled to the hallway and leaned toward the living room. "Did you eat?"

"No." He squirmed against the cushions and arched his back. "Fix me something, will you?"

She bit her lip. If she made a sandwich for herself, how much more work was it to make two? As she built the sandwiches, her mind reviewed what had happened with Julia. She'd stopped with no plans, but the fragile woman's image had drawn her there. Instead of being a support for Julia, she'd leaned on her with her own problems and told her the deepest wounds she'd felt—the loss of her mother and Doug's betrayal. That's what it felt like. He'd hidden a secret life of gambling and carousing, threw away their finances and then when it got too deep, he dug his own grave. Suicide. What could be more desperate? Cowardly.

She'd never thought of it like that. She'd had her down moments, but she found courage to build herself up, to make things better. Yes, she'd failed at times, but she'd grasped hold of what she could—even her bootstraps—and found a way to make life better.

Dying at his own hand showed weakness, but without seeking God's help, weakness meant giving up, facing he couldn't do it alone. As Steph read the Bible, she understood why Molly and Nick could fight battles with perseverance and how they could have hope even when a situation seemed hopeless.

Right now, when she thought of Hal, his attitude seemed hopeless, but it didn't have to be. If she prayed—hearing her refer to prayer sounded alien—the Bible said God would hear her. Though uncomfortable, Steph closed her eyes and prayed.

When she finished, she carried Hal's sandwich to the living room. He hadn't moved. "Nick's dropping by. Do you want him to think you haven't left the spot since the last time he saw you?"

"I don't care what he thinks." He raised his head from the sofa arm.

She jerked back from his attitude. "What's wrong with Nick?"

Hal squirmed and adjusted the pillow he'd pushed beneath his neck. "One of those dudes who's out for something."

"Out for what? He's never asked for a thing." She shook her head.

"I can tell. I'm good at reading people."

She monitored an indignant snort. So was she, and what she read about Hal wasn't good, but she didn't want to even go there. His attitude disappointed her. "In this house, you'll respect my guests."

He raised his head, his blond hair tousled from the pillow, and grabbed the remote, then snapped off the TV and sat up. "I'm up. Now what?"

"Say thanks for the sandwich." Steph had all she could do but scream.

He rolled his eyes. "Thanks. Should I kiss your feet?"

You should get a job. The words blasted through her mind. "Have you looked for work?"

"I bought a newspaper." His arm swung toward a folded paper under the lamp table. "Nothing I'm qualified for."

What did he qualify for? Her body shook with frustration. She couldn't listen anymore. "I'm out tonight. Did you remember?"

He frowned.

"I'm in a wedding." She didn't ask what caused his upset. He probably expected her to cook dinner. "Let me know when Nick comes."

Inside her bedroom, Steph looked at her watch. If Nick didn't arrive soon, she'd be gone. She pulled her dress from the closet, wrapped in the clear plastic cover. The color brightened her thoughts as she slipped on her undergarments, happy that she'd taken her shower in the morning. No time to dawdle now.

Wrapped in a bathrobe, she slipped into her bathroom and opened the drawer where she stored her cosmetics. She checked through her blush and lipstick colors for corals or pastel melon shades to match her dress.

The telephone rang, and before she could reach it, the ringing stopped. She stood beside her bedside table, waiting. Hal's voice blasted down the hall, and she picked up the receiver.

"Sorry, Steph. I had to run an errand, and now I'm hung up in traffic. When are you leaving?"

"In a few minutes. Don't worry about it. I didn't cancel my ride with Molly's sister."

"Oh."

Disappointment sounded in his voice, but she'd come to know that she couldn't count on Nick, at least not for being on time. "It's better this way. I'll see you at the wedding."

Though she accepted his excuse, his apology haunted her. In the short time they'd known each other, the word *sorry* seemed as common as hello. She slipped the phone into the stand and returned to the mirror. A little eye shadow, mascara and lipstick finished the job. She tossed a skirt and top over her head, then sat on the bed, thinking about Nick.

She saw so much good in him, and he could be counted on for so many things. He'd resolved the fence problem, he'd rescued her from Martin, he'd appeared so many times with fun ideas—picnics, walking the dogs in the park, playing with Fred. He'd even asked her to the wedding. Thinking of going alone had been a bummer. And most of all, he'd kissed her.

Her hand rose on its own and pressed her lips. Doug had stopped kissing her long before he'd died. Nick's kiss had awakened her to the truth. She wanted to work through her lack of confidence and guilt she'd been left with and be healed. She wanted a life. She wanted to be married one day, and she dreamed it could be to Nick.

But the idea filled her with fear—fear of disappointment, fear of being hurt, fear of never gaining the love she wanted so badly. Nick had helped her realize what life could be. She'd begun to feel whole again.

When she returned to the living room, she spotted her handbag and realized she'd forgotten to transfer items to her evening bag. As she picked it up, Hal looked at her from his usual spot on the couch. "Mr. Rich Guy isn't coming so I figured I had permission to recline."

"Hal, don't be so critical. Please." She clutched her handbag to her chest to stop herself from throwing it at him. "What do you have against Nick?"

"I don't trust him."

She reeled backward. "You don't trust him. Why?"

"He wants something, and it's not you. He doesn't respect you."

The comment prickled on her neck.

"If he cared, he'd be here. Since I've come, he's been late or hasn't shown up more than he's arrived on time."

She didn't have to answer to Hal, and for someone who hadn't lifted his finger to help her, he had no room to talk respect. "What do you think he wants?"

"I don't know. Your money."

Money? She sank to the edge of an easy chair. "Hal, you didn't listen to me when I talked to you the other day."

"I listened, but I don't believe it."

She shrugged and rose. "Believe what you want." She shook her head, amazed at his belligerence, and headed back to her room to find her evening bag. Steph located her clutch in the bottom drawer of the dresser. She transferred what she would need, then tossed in the lipstick shade she'd chosen. Before she dropped in her cell phone, she turned it to vibrate. No way did she want that to interrupt the wedding.

Money. Steph grabbed the coin purse from the bag, then pulled her driver's license from her wallet and opened the bill slot to grab a few bills. As she did, an uneasy feeling swept over her. She'd been certain she had a few twenties along with smaller bills when she was at the salon, but now she had only one. Her mind flew back to the salon. She'd charged her hairstyling and tipped with cash. Where had she left her handbag? On her hair-stylists' stand, then by her feet when she sat beneath the dryer. She was certain.

A car's honk stopped her thoughts. Molly's sister. She tossed a few dollars into the change purse and shoved her handbag in the closet. She'd think about it later. With her dress over her arm, she hurried to the front door, waved goodbye to Hal and strode to the car.

A soft breeze ruffled her skirt. She looked up at the clear sky. Perfect. Tonight Molly's dream would come true.

Dreams. What might happen to hers?

Chapter Eight

Nick eyed himself in the mirror. Suit, white shirt and tie. He'd even taken time to shine his shoes. Nick glanced at his watch. He had plenty of time. Steph would be pleased. Although sitting alone was the pits, he knew later Steph would join him at the reception. Even though she had her brides-maid duties to perform, which she reminded him numerous times, he would enjoy her company when she'd finished.

Tonight he hoped they might have time to talk—really talk. Their kiss lingered in his mind. He wanted to tell her how he felt about her. Even about Fred. Though he tried to control his feelings, even tried to convince himself a relationship with a woman wouldn't work for him, his emotions tangled around her in some kind of illusive excuse that she needed his help. Too quickly he'd learned that Steph handled her life with solid footing. She didn't need him. Not really. Now imagination had taken over his good sense. And he was tired of make-believe.

He glanced one more time at his image in the mirror, then headed for the door. As he turned the knob, he hesitated. Veering back to his desk, he picked up the wedding card with his blessings at the bottom along with a check. Brent Runyan didn't need money, but what did a single guy buy a couple who'd already established their homes? They didn't need another waffle iron. He slipped the card into an inside pocket and strode to his car.

Saturday traffic seemed heavier than usual, but he'd left plenty of time to arrive with a half hour to spare. His bad habit had to end. The late afternoon sun filtered through the window, and he turned on the air-conditioning. Evening would cool and be a prefect setting for their reception—and a classy one at that. He'd been to a few events at Oakland Hills Country Club. He'd even had the opportunity to see a major PGA tournament there. His wedding plans with Cara had been simpler and definitely less expensive.

A light turned red ahead, and Nick put his foot on the brake and slowed. As he came to a stop, his cell phone buzzed in his suit coat pocket. He grasped it and checked the caller. Martin. Martin hadn't called for anything since they'd had words. Nick's chest constricted as his mother's image filled his thoughts. He pressed the phone against his ear. "What's wrong? Is Mom—"

"She's fine, Nick. I hate to do this, but I can't get home for a few more hours. This shindig is dragging on. Is there any way you can drive by and check on Suzette? She's been tearing things up when I'm late, and I'm sure she needs to go outside by now."

Nick gripped the steering wheel. "I'm on my way to a wedding. I can't be—"

"It'll take a minute, Nick. I hate to ask, but—"

Only a minute. How often had he heard that? Nick eyed his watch and stretched his mouth to relax his jaw. "If I'm late for this wedding, I'll be…" He shook his head. "Okay, Martin, but I'll be in and out of there in a minute."

"Fine. I appreciate it."

Nick hung up, wishing he'd said no, but his thought wasn't with Martin but Suzette. She didn't like being home for lengths of time alone. He hoped that might improve with some training.

He made a right turn at the light, then turned around and headed back. Martin's house was only a mile away. A quick run outside for Suzette, and he'd be on his way again. He twisted his wrist and checked the time. No problem. He'd still make it before the wedding march.

* * *

Canon in D filled the church as Steph inched down the aisle, the way they showed her at the rehearsal. If she had her way, she'd run down and get it over with. Molly should be the one taking her merry old time and enjoying every moment. For Steph, the ceremony evoked memories she wanted to escape. The hope she'd felt at her wedding—the wonder, the anticipation of how her life would smooth away the sadness—had caused her pulse to throb and her spirit lift. With her past behind her, Steph knew the warning signs, and she knew Molly's life had been guided by God's blessing. She'd watched it unfold, and finally, she'd begun to understand.

The guests seated in the pews craned their necks to look at Molly, waiting in the back—relatives and friends, mainly in pairs. She had dreaded tonight when she thought she'd be alone, without anyone to share the evening.

Nick's face loomed in her thoughts. He'd answered a prayer she hadn't asked God, although she'd wished it so often. Perhaps God heard wishes and sensed they were prayers. She still had so much to learn and so much to understand, but her heart had opened in a new way. Now she hungered to learn more.

Steph wished she'd known God all her life.

She'd been raised in a home where God hadn't played a part, although she had blurred memories of her mother attending church alone once in a while. Steph's mother tried, in her own way, to be a good mother, but more than not, Steph had felt alone. Her father came home from work late. When she became a teen, her mother had taken a job, and her tiredness meant living on fast food. Then, her mother had grown silent. Yet she tried to listen to her children's needs. On weekends, her father gathered with friends to play cards, eating pizza and drinking beer. Steph missed a sense of family, and she missed the tenderness.

The organ music covered her thoughts and pulled her back. When she reached the front, she turned and faced Molly's sister, Stacy, who glided down the aisle dressed in a coral gown, a darker hue than Steph's pastel shade. They both carried mixed spring flowers and each wore the gold chain and delicate floral charm that Molly had presented them with for being her attendants.

Facing the congregation, she let her gaze wander down the rows of guests, hoping to spot Nick. She couldn't wait to see him in a suit. Though he'd sometimes worn sport coats when he dropped by, she could only imagine how handsome he'd be today.

Her attempt to scan the guests ended when Stacy reached her side, and Steph knew the bride would be next. She caught Brent's gaze, his eyes glowing as if he'd waited for this moment all his life.

The music shifted to a triumphant march. The congregation stood, and ahead of her, Molly, on her father's arm, moved down the aisle, her satin gown draped softly to the ground with a veil in a matching design; beneath the veil, Molly's flawless face—that creamy youthful skin that she'd always envied—radiated her happiness. She'd found her soul mate. She'd found the man that Molly said the Lord had created just for her.

A flutter ran through Steph's chest. Nick's glinting eyes and full mouth curving in a playful smile warmed her. She searched the guests again with no sign of Nick. She focused on Molly as her father and mother gave her away. Brent took her arm, and as they stepped forward, Steph scanned the crowd one more time before she turned, disappointed.

Nick pulled into Martin's driveway and rushed inside. The silence struck him when he called for Suzette. No response. Normally the dog greeted him at the door. He paused at the living-room archway. Toss pillows lay on the carpet, one with some stuffing visible near a seam. He squinted. Maybe a tear.

"Suzette?" The quiet disturbed him as he sprinted to the kitchen. A trash can lay on its side, its contents strewn across the floor. "Suzette?"

His gaze flew to the outside door. Closed.

A whimper captured his attention, and he skidded around the kitchen island. His heart stopped as he fell to the floor on his knees. Suzette lay on her side, drool dripping from her mouth to the floor with streaks of red. Her labored breathing drove his pulse higher.

He eyed the trash. Chicken bones. His concern turned to fear. He tried to look in her throat, but she wouldn't let him pry open her mouth. Instead, he lifted Suzette into his arms, placed his fists beneath her rib cage and compressed her abdomen and released it three times. The dog's deep rumble and sharp cry stopped him.

With no room for error, he grabbed his cell and hit Martin's number. He needed to find the dog's veterinarian. Any animal hospital. The ring went into voice mail. Nick dropped the phone into his pocket, then tore through the cabinet where he thought Martin kept the phone book. His fingers trembled as he flashed through pages. Upholsterers. Vacation rentals. Veterinarians. His pulse raced. He scanned the listings. Rochester, finally. Crooks Road.

Suzette's shallow breathing filled him with terror. He drew in a breath and hoisted the dog in his arms. Her ninety pounds of deadweight caused Nick to stagger, but he found his bearing as he ran down the hallway and outside, shutting the door and hoping it locked. He managed to open the SUV door, laid Suzette inside and jumped into the driver's seat.

"Hang in there, Suzette." His eyes blurred as he headed down the street, fearing the worst but praying a blessing.

As the pastor spoke, Steph's gaze rose to the stained-glass window, depicting a risen Jesus. His index finger pointing upward as if extending peace to the world. Peace. Did faith provide peace? Peace would be a gift. Steph longed to feel complete.

She lowered her eyes and realized Molly and Brent had stepped closer to the minister. His words washed over her, words about faithfulness and cooperation, words of encouragement and Scripture that stated man and woman should not be alone.

Their vows were spoken and Brent's nephew Randy, almost thirteen, handed him the rings for the exchange. Molly's diamond glistened in the church light as Brent slipped the band on her finger, studded with a row of twinkling diamonds.

Prayers rose, and Steph listened, joining in the hope for a truly blessed and solid marriage for her two friends. And a family, something she'd never had. Brent had raised Randy following the tragic death of the boy's father, and Molly had been a great influence on him. Molly would make a wonderful mother.

With the final kiss, music resounded from the organ with Ode to Joy. Molly and Brent recessed down the aisle watched by family and friends whose faces shone with happiness. Steph searched the crowd, hoping to find Nick's smiling eyes while emotions battled within her. Late again or had something happened?

An icy fear shivered down her back. Nick had a problem with being late, but not always, and this event was important. She longed to slip away from the receiving line and look at her cell phone. He may have called.

Or maybe not if something serious…

The possibility unsettled her, and she pressed a smile to her face, hoping Molly wouldn't see the truth.

One by one the guests filed past and made their way to the parking lot and their cars where they would head for the reception. Steph made a sharp turn, aiming toward her cell phone.

"The photographer's waiting."

A voice cut through her distraction, and she followed the others back down the aisle where they posed and smiled, posed and smiled. Her smile felt like clown makeup, a smile on the outside with heartbreak inside.

Steph glanced at her watch. How many more photographs?

Relief came as she hurried back to the bride's room. Her purse lay beneath the skirt she'd worn to the church. She shifted the coin purse and pulled out her cell phone. When she flipped it open, she read "One missed message." Her heart raced as she pressed the button and heard Nick's voice.

"Steph. It's a long story, but I'm at the vet's with Suzette. She's going to be okay, I think, and I finally got hold of Martin. He's on his way here, then I'll leave. I'll see you at the reception and tell you about it."

Suzette? Steph's mind conjured what might have happened. Her concern shifted from Nick to Suzette, then back to Nick.

She would plaster on a smile until she learned what had happened. She talked to herself and hoped that God would hear her. She wasn't certain if he knew her name.

Relief filled Nick once he rolled down the long driveway of Oakland Hills Country Club. Though his thoughts clung to Suzette, he couldn't help but admire the club's sweeping green lawn and white columns stretching along the lengthy entrance of the building. The grandeur could intimidate the most confident individual.

Nick entered the elegant windowed foyer as the sound of a string ensemble drew him toward the spacious dining room. Through the windows, a veranda extended along the rolling hills of the fairways, spotted with floral gardens and trees. Nick didn't fit in this elegant setting. Though his business might one day grow to allow him to pay the membership fee, he would never feel a part of this.

A table near the door held name cards placed in small silver picture frames. He found his name among the ones still there. Table seven. Before moving on, he located the bridal table and looked for Steph. He hoped she'd gotten his message rather than think he was late again because he was thoughtless. Disappointed he couldn't see her, Nick edged his way through the chairs and guests until he located his table. To his relief, he recognized a familiar face.

Frank Capatelli, Brent's company business manager, rose and extended his hand. "Good to see you, Nick."

Nick grasped his palm with a welcome shake before he was introduced to Frank's wife and two others at the table. When he settled into a chair, he eyed the bridal table again. Steph still wasn't there. He sipped ice water from crystal stemware as he scanned the guests, hoping he'd see her among them. Finally, he spotted the groom and excused himself. Brent Runyan turned as Nick approached, and his face spread to a smile. Nick extended his hand. "Congratulations, and thanks for inviting me."

Brent clasped his shoulder and gave it a shake. "Thanks for coming. I hear you know Molly's friend Steph."

"I do." He craned his neck again. "Where is she?"

Brent glanced toward his table, then scanned the guests. "The girls went to comb their hair, I think." His eyebrows raised and he gestured toward the dais. "Molly's back. She's beckoning me to the table. Dinner's about to be served. I'm sure you'll have a chance to say hello to Molly after dinner." He gave his shoulder another pat and made his way to the bridal-party table.

Nick sank back into his seat, longing to talk with Steph, but spoons clinked on china, and Nick looked up to catch Brent give Molly a sweet kiss. Soon the toasts began. Listening to the best man, Nick's gaze swept to Steph, his pulse running a race. She looked amazing. He tried to catch her eye, but hers were directed at the best man. He shook his head, disappointed.

When she rose to join in the best man's toast, Nick had a better look. Besides the mass of curls Nick had never seen before, Steph looked beautiful. Draped in a soft fabric the color of medium-rare steak, she took his breath away. Her floor-length gown draped over her shoulders to a V-like neck-line, then fell in soft folds from her waist where a satin row of bands accentuated her slender figure.

His stomach twitched as he pulled his gaze from her and tried to concentrate on the conversation. His knee jiggled, waiting for the moment she left the head table or he could approach her and tell her what happened.

Nick's knee bounced beneath the shrimp-colored tablecloth, but he managed to lean back in his chair, making small talk with Frank and his friends while the food arrived at the table. A deli-cious array of family-style dishes were served—prime rib, chicken, pasta. Brent had outdone himself. But Nick's appetite waned. All he could think about was Steph.

With frustration rising, Nick stood and excused himself, then maneuvered around the dinner tables to the bridal party seated on a dais. Although he felt like an idiot, he pushed past the last table and stood in front of Steph.

She sliced a piece of chicken, lifted her fork and then lowered it as her face broke into a beaming smile. "Nick. I was worried." She searched his eyes. "Is Suzette okay?"

"She should be fine. I'll give you details later." He stood a moment, feeling his chest expand and the thudding of his beating heart. "I wanted you to know I'm here."

"I'm glad. Relieved." Steph extended her hand toward him. He grasped her fingers and gave them a squeeze. "I'll be done here soon."

He nodded, hating to let go of her hand. "I'm over there." He gestured to his table, then released her hand and returned to his dinner. Maybe now he could enjoy the meal.

Chapter Nine

Steph stepped down from the dais and headed toward Nick's table. Her mouth felt dry, and she longed for a drink. Tonic with lime if they had it. She liked the refreshing tang. Steph squeezed her way into the throng of Molly's friends and family. When she neared Nick's table, she realized he wasn't there. Stopping at the bar, she ordered her drink, then made her way to the sidelines to find a place to wait, but her gaze was drawn to the wide windows of the dining room.

The sun hung low in the sky, adorned by a magnificent sunset. Steph drew closer, admiring the display of color. She scanned the area for Nick. No sight of him. A quick look outside wouldn't hurt. She sought a door and stepped out to the veranda. The well-groomed grass spread across the expanse dotted with sand traps and lighter-hued greens. To her left, she noticed an island of spring flowers rising in colorful tiers of daisies, purple heather and multi-hued impatiens. Beautiful.

A shadow fell beside her, and before she turned, a hand brushed her arm. She spun around, her heart flitting against her breastbone.

"Nick." She warmed to his touch. "I looked for you."

His lips curved into a welcoming smile. "I was talking with Brent in the lobby." He gave a toss of his head toward the festivity inside. "This is quite a celebration."

"Weddings always are." Their eyes met and didn't move. "I'm glad you're here."

"So am I." His gaze searched her face and lingered on her hair. "I love your curls. You should wear it that way more often."

"Thanks. I—"

"Steph, I'm so sorry for missing the wedding."

Her pulse skipped at his serious countenance. "What happened?"

He shook his head and told her the details. "By the time Martin arrived, I knew Suzette would be okay, but they are keeping her overnight to take a look at her throat in the morning. The swelling was bad and blocked her air passage. I guess a dog's throat is delicate and can be damaged, but if the swelling goes down by morning, she can come home."

"I'm so glad." Steph pictured the injured dog, and she imagined the horrible sight Nick had found when he reached her. She would send Martin a card to let him know her concern. "You must have been a mess."

"I was a wreck. I never realized how much that dog means to me until that moment. I'd thought about heading back home and not coming, but—" he pressed his hand against her cheek "— seeing you now, I'm glad I changed my mind."

She cupped his hand with her palm. "I'm glad you did, too."

He broke his gaze and gestured toward the sky. "Amazing."

She viewed the horizon. "It's lovely. I've never seen anything quite so beautiful."

"I have."

His words touched her as a whisper, and goose-flesh sprinkled up along her arms. When she turned toward him, his eyes spoke to her. She answered him the same way. His head lowered and his lips touched hers. Though her mind battled against falling in love, today she raised a white flag and surrendered. He moved his mouth against hers as a ripple of longing shivered through her. This is what she yearned for, a love that offers laughter, support and completeness.

His hand swept along her arm, the warmth taking

way the chill of the breeze and the cold fear that had lived in her heart for so long. Could she ever be the same without him?

Nick drew back, his eyes searching hers. She had no answers, but for once in her life, she had hope. His gaze washed over her and paused on her gown. He shook his head, then motioned to the sky. "You're part of the sunset."

Steph melted as a wave of emotion swept through her. She managed to shift her attention to the merging colors spilling across the horizon in golds, oranges, corals, then to the soft hue of her gown. No words entered her mind.

An evening breeze swept along the veranda, sending a chill down her bare arms.

"You're cold." He drew his arm from his jacket.

Steph stopped him. "We can go inside. It is getting cool with the sun going down."

Nick slipped his arm back into the sleeve and straightened his lapel, then curved his arm around her shoulder and guided her toward the door.

A cozy warmth wrapped around her, chasing away the old feelings of loneliness.

At the doorway, music vibrated through the windows. The band played a romantic song, and as they stepped inside, dancers glided across the parquet floor. Steph set her empty glass on a tray, her gaze on Nick to see what he might do now.

He slipped his arm from her shoulder and captured her hand. "How about a fresh drink?"

She agreed, and he led her past the dance floor, only letting her hand go when he stepped up to the bar. His thoughtfulness touched her more than his offer to let her use his jacket.

She studied him as he ordered their soft drinks. She'd never seen him in a suit, and the vision etched in her mind. He wore a suit well, a dark gray with a white shirt and a tie colored in a slate tone. The line broadened his shoulders and accentuated his trim physique.

Nick pivoted and handed her the glass, then pressed his palm against her arm and guided her away from the crowd. They wandered past the dance floor into a small nook with a few tall tables and high stools. The music drifted in from the hall, providing a pleasant background.

"Let's sit." He motioned to the seats.

Steph scooted onto the stool and set her glass on the table, turning it and watching the light refract in the facets of the base. She sensed Nick watching her, and when she looked up, he greeted her with a tender smile.

"You look amazing."

Her palm swept across the soft folds of her gown as she gained courage to admit her attraction. "You're pretty handsome yourself."

He flicked his lapel. "This old thing?"

His playful comment eased her mind, and she sipped her drink. "I wonder if Suzette has separation anxiety. Have you talked with Martin about obedience training? Molly can help him with that, too."

A puff of air shot from his nose. "I mentioned it, but the conversation veered away to another topic." He looked away a moment, then turned back. "I'll be honest. We were arguing so I never had a serious talk with him, but I did mention it."

Picturing Nick arguing seemed unreal. Even the way he rescued her from Martin's anger, he approached his brother with humor and gentleness. "I hope it wasn't about Fred."

"About many things." For a moment, he'd settled into thought. "I learned one thing that surprised me that day."

Steph waited, hesitating to ask. When the time stretched, she spoke. "You don't have to tell me."

"Tell you?" He gave her a quizzical look, then understanding lit his face. "Sorry, I was thinking. I learned that he plans to breed Suzette."

"Breed her." A weight fell to her shoulders. "She's a beautiful dog, but the world has so many homeless animals. I wish people would give a home to those first. They might not all be purebred, but some of them are great dogs."

He nodded. "I know. I saw a handful of them at the shelter. It's heartbreaking"

The look on his face made her weak. She loved his sensitivity. Yet he saw it as a weakness. She didn't understand that.

His hand balled into a fist and plopped onto the table. "Martin doesn't think of others."

"But you do." That's one thing he could never deny.

His expression relaxed. "I try to." He caught her gaze and sent her a sweet grin.

The relaxing moment wrapped around her like his hug. They could talk and discuss things with mutual respect. She'd never had that after she married. Steph pushed her glass aside and glanced through the archway to the festivities. She hoped Molly didn't need her for anything, because she was enjoying these moments with Nick.

Nick dropped from the stool. "Can I get you something else?"

His look sent prickles down her arms. "Maybe later. Thanks."

He tilted his head toward the couples swaying to the music. "Would you like to dance?"

Her heart stood still. She hadn't danced in years and she wasn't sure she remembered how.

Nick didn't wait for an answer. He placed his hand beneath her elbow as she lowered herself from the stool, then guided her to the dance floor. His arm slipped around her waist, and his hand captured her palm. He drew her close, his feet gliding to the music as hers followed without error. Maybe she hadn't forgotten after all. As they moved across the floor, an astounding feeling of oneness rolled through her. How long had it been since she felt whole?

The music segued from one love song to another, and Nick drew her even closer, his hand warm against the small of her back, his strong fingers guiding her to move and sway with the slow rhythm. Her heart sang louder than the concern that beat like an unwanted drum in her subconscious. She'd wanted to be friends, nothing more, but tonight she admitted her feelings had sailed away and her heart with them.

She'd settled on a life alone. Romantic thoughts of love had been warped by her marital struggles and had died with Doug. The idea of another relationship felt like a dark shadow. But meeting Nick cast light on her future. Then hope slipped from the locked recesses of her heart, and now the deep emotions frightened her. Trusting someone again took confidence and faith, attributes she wasn't sure she had. Nick's strong Christian beliefs influenced his thoughts and actions. Could he accept her as she was, a woman longing to know Jesus as he did, but not knowing how?

Nick's breath whispered against her cheek. He held her in his arms, swaying to the music and making her feel worthy. She enjoyed the melody filling the room, a lovely song with words that stirred her heart. It would linger in her mind tomorrow, bringing her back to this moment.

Wasn't hope like that? It played over and over in her mind like a memorable tune, drawing her to reach out for things that seemed impossible. But for the first time in years, maybe they were. Somewhere she'd heard that with God all things are possible.

Her hope came from the heart, but she'd lived with her head for too many years. Logic and reason. Falling for someone she'd only met a month earlier proffered no reality. Reality was true. What about hope?

When the song ended, Nick guided Steph from the dance floor, wondering what had happened. Her kiss had been warm, and she'd moved easily on the dance floor until he'd felt her tense. Though her expression hadn't wavered, something had caused her to withdraw for a moment. Had he held her too close? He didn't think so. But something had gone wrong.

His experience with women fell short. Dating sat on his list with organizing his pantry and cleaning his storage closet. It didn't happen. He'd stacked and pushed items from one spot to another until he couldn't find a thing.

Dating fit right in with his "things to do one day" list. Women appeared in his life with encouraging smiles, but no one had captured his attention until Steph came along, and she did it without trying. His company needed his undivided attention and took the bulk of his resources.

Then tonight Brent initiated some business and talked about an order he planned to send in that would be a boon. That was the kind of large order his business needed.

Yet his concern didn't end with his company or finances. He wanted to understand himself and figure out where he'd gone wrong with Cara. Each time he saw Steph, his feelings grew. He lost sight of reality, and his heart took over. That scared him. But he didn't want to lose her. Martin's comment about Cara struck him often. Had she really expected too much?

Steph's arm brushed against his, and her expression let him know he'd drifted off in thought too long. He clasped her arm above the elbow. "Let's check the dessert table."

Her full lips tilted to a grin, and she looked relaxed again.

He wanted to be honest, but finding the courage took strength, and he didn't know if he had enough.

He guided her to a display of cookies and slices of fruit-drenched cheesecakes. Though he wasn't one bit hungry, he grasped a napkin and selected a cookie.

Steph studied the desserts. "I'll just have coffee." She patted her slender tummy as if she were too full.

She looked perfect. Too perfect.

Steph strode to the coffee urn, poured a cup, then doctored it to her taste and swung around to face him.

His table had emptied when he returned, and Nick scanned the crowd. "The others are dancing." He motioned to the dance floor, then pulled out the chair beside his and held it as she sat.

The muted light turned her gown to a deeper coral and brought out the colors in her skin. A wistful expression caused her to look ethereal like the *Mona Lisa*'s secret smile. He longed to know what drew her away sometimes when they talked.

"We've become so close this past month." Mundane comment. He had no idea why he'd said it.

The color in her cheeks deepened. "It seems much longer."

His pulse gave a tug. "I hope that's good."

"It is, and it's odd. I usually take a long time getting comfortable with people, but you're different."

Different. He could relate to that. She'd affected him more than he could put into words. "Unique. That's what you are. A unique woman."

"I think I'm supposed to say thanks." Her grin faded. "I've been thinking about that."

That? "You mean, being unique?"

"No. About us." She turned her head slowly and studied him.

Air drained from Nick's lungs. An overwhelming concern struck him. What if he led her on to think their relationship could be more than he could offer right now? What if she wanted to end their friendship?

"You look upset." Steph's smooth brow had furrowed.

Nick's head jerked toward her. "I'm…hoping I haven't done anything to—"

"You've done nothing, Nick, except be who you are."

Late. The word flashed through his mind. But he wanted to work on that. Before he made reference to being late again, her comment struck him. Be who you are. "I'd love to know who I am, Steph. That's one of the things I talked about with Martin." The admission spilled into the air, but the comment didn't phase her. She looked miles away.

She stared into the coffee cup. "I've lived on the edge of life for a long time, and recently—since I met you—I'm actually living again."

"You went through a bad time when your

husband died. I know it takes years to paste yourself back together."

A spark of surprise lit her eyes. "Have you ever felt like that?"

Felt? He'd eaten the paste and it tasted awful. "I have."

She looked at him as if waiting for him to elaborate. Instead he felt tense. Before he could wrap his tongue around words, he heard a rustle behind him and glanced over his shoulder.

"Molly." Steph's voice broke the silence. "I hope I didn't miss something I was supposed to be doing."

She grinned. "No. You haven't missed a thing." She waved her hand across the room. "I'm trying to follow Brent to meet all his associates, but I haven't had a chance to talk with you since the church." She shifted toward Nick. "Nice to see you again."

He rose. "You've put on a great party, Molly. I pray you and Brent have a long and happy life together."

"Thanks, Nick." She grasped his arm and gave it a squeeze, then looked toward the dance floor. "Looks like I have to stop socializing. Already. I'm being summoned…by my husband." She giggled. "I love hearing that." She sent them a grin and hurried off.

Nick grasped the chair back, watching her. "She looks happy."

"She's happier than I've ever seen her."

His breath hitched, hearing melancholy in Steph's voice. He couldn't imagine what she'd gone through losing her husband. Losing Cara couldn't be compared to the loss of a mate. He shifted his eyes toward Steph, his pulse skipping again when he saw the cascade of curls spiraling to her shoulders.

She brushed a ringlet from her cheek as if she'd read his mind, then turned his way. "It's probably time for the bridal dance."

Nick moved back to his chair, his mind tumbling back to their conversation before Molly arrived. Sometimes Steph had seemed lonely. He'd often wondered if she'd had a good marriage. If he could guarantee he'd be a good husband, the thought of marriage wouldn't worry him so much.

Marriage? What happened to the friendship he and Steph had been talking about? How did marriage slip into his thoughts? He scanned the festivities. A wedding reception. Naturally marriage would come to mind.

He searched for something to say as they sat in silence. He suspected Steph was doing the same. They both had things to discuss, but tonight having a serious talk wasn't going to happen. Another time and place made more sense.

Her absorbed expression vanished, and he turned toward the dance floor to see what was happening.

The couples from his table were returning. Nick eyed the activity, suspecting it was time for some of the typical wedding traditions.

Steph tilted her head. "Molly's beckoning to me. I'm not sure if she wants me or both of us." She stepped behind Nick, then rested her hand on his shoulder. "Looks like she's throwing the bouquet." She backed up and returned to her chair, resting her hands on the back. "I'm not going."

Nick shifted so he could see Molly. Her wave was obvious. "She wants you, Steph."

Tension showed on her face as Steph closed her eyes. "I'm supposed to join the unmarried women hoping to catch the bouquet."

Though she took a step forward, Nick could see her mouth, "Do I have to?"

Molly's head bounced in a determined nod.

She looked defeated. "I have to do this."

"Go ahead. I'm right behind you."

Though Steph crept forward, she stayed in the back fringes of the women, and Nick planted his feet a few steps behind her, encouraging her to move closer for Molly's sake.

Steph didn't budge.

Nick never understood those traditions, and Steph made it clear what she thought of the practice.

When Molly turned her back to those waiting, she dipped so low Nick lost sight of her behind the throng. The DJ began. One. Two. Three. Molly rose like a catapult, and the bouquet sailed above the heads of the women.

Steph spun around while Nick tried to back away, but the bouquet landed in his arms.

A burst of laughter filled the air as he rushed forward with the flowers and slipped them into Steph's arms. "These were meant for you."

Steph's startled expression melted as she broke into laughter.

A warm flush rose to his cheeks, and he watched her gaze at the flowers, then back to him. "You caught it, and you know what this means?"

He nodded, his embarrassment growing.

"Congratulations." She sidled up to him with the bouquet. "Who's the lucky lady?"

Nick bit his tongue, jarred by the name that flew into his mind. "Wouldn't you like to know?" He managed a lighthearted smile, then headed back to the table. He felt safer there.

When he reached it, he pulled out Steph's chair, but when he looked up, he saw the photographer nab her. She gave Nick a shrug and followed the man back to the dance floor where they were preparing to do something. The garter toss, he guessed.

Nick made a quick getaway and headed for the restroom. He'd already snatched the bouquet. He definitely had no interest in catching the garter.

Chapter Ten

Steph cuddled the new cocker spaniel. Its wet tongue dragged across her cheek, and her heart burst. "Here. Take him back, or I'll be tempted." She handed the dog to Emily.

"That's what I was hoping." Emily released a faint smile, which was rare for her.

Steph always wondered why. The young woman usually wore faded jeans and a baggy T-shirt, and though she appeared to be in her early twenties, her body language signaled an older woman. "Your job here is only part time, right?"

The cocker squirmed in Emily's arms, and she cuddled it to her, both of them looking a little lost. "Molly said she hopes to let me work full time soon."

"That's great." But something about Emily left Steph wondering. "You must work somewhere else, too."

"I'm a dog sitter."

Steph drew back. "Really? You mean, you live in people's—"

"Not always. I have a studio apartment so I enjoy staying in homes, but I walk people's dogs and care for them when they're away from home. Vacations or some people work long hours." She shrugged. "You know."

"That's an interesting job, and you make life easier for pet owners."

"I hope so." She gave Steph one of her serious looks.

As she shifted the cocker in her arms, Steph's stomach smacked her heart. A thick scar marred each of Emily's wrists as if she'd… No. Her mind flew back to Doug, then withdrew as she peered at the scars again.

Emily's face blanched as she stepped away. "I need to—"

"Don't go."

The woman's eyes widened, and she curled her arms around the puppy to hide her scars. "Why?"

"Because I need to talk with you." She searched Emily's face, hoping she could learn something, anything that would resolve the endless doubts that struck her so unexpectedly after she'd thought she'd healed.

"About what?" A frightened look etched her face as her eyes lowered to her wrists.

Steph had opened the door, and she couldn't walk away now. "My husband committed suicide, Emily. Four years ago." An icy chill shuddered through her bones, realizing this woman had considered such a horrible death. She gave a quick nod to Emily's wrists. "Did you—"

Emily's eyes closed. "Yes. A couple years ago." She lifted her eyelids, her face mottled.

Steph cringed, having dredged up the woman's sorrow for her own selfish motive. "I shouldn't ask you, but—"

Emily rested her hand on Steph's arm. "It's okay." Her gentle eyes probed Steph's and her color returned. "You want to know what you could have done and if you were the cause."

"I want to understand so I can let it go."

Emily patted her arm. "I need to return to the office, but we can talk before you leave." She nestled the puppy to her cheek. "He should be put down so he can adjust."

"Later's fine. Thank you." Steph watched her plod back to the pens, then headed to the door to check on the dogs playing outside.

The sun's rays warmed the chill she'd felt seeing the evidence of Emily's attempt to take her life. What caused that kind of emptiness? Steph admitted she'd felt lonely and incomplete since Doug's death, even as difficult as marriage had been, but she would never have taken her life. The depth of hopelessness seemed—

Her cell phone sounded. Steph drew it from her pocket and read the caller's name. Her pulse did a jig when she heard Nick's voice.

"What about getting together tonight?"

Did he mean a date? Walking the dogs?

"Steph?"

"What did you have in mind?" Fred distracted her. He flashed past, sashaying around the yard with Miranda, a mixed breed, German shepherd and Samoyed.

"Let's go to Detroit. Hart Plaza. The RiverWalk."

The RiverWalk. She hadn't seen it since it had been expanded.

"Maybe have dinner down there. Someplace with music. What do you say?"

He'd also called to let her know Suzette had recovered and was home; Steph hadn't seen him since the wedding. She missed him, and it bothered her that she felt so attached. "It sounds nice."

"Great. I'll pick you up at six-thirty."

She agreed and hung up, certain that the talk they'd started at the wedding would continue on the RiverWalk. She needed to decide what to do. Was she ready to talk about herself?

By late afternoon, Steph wondered if the day would ever end. Though she anticipated her evening with Nick, her eagerness to talk with Emily remained the pinnacle of her thoughts. As she eyed her watch, she feared Emily had forgotten. With the dog's owners arriving to take their animals home, she couldn't find time to remind her.

As the last dog trotted away with its owner, Emily appeared at her doorway. She left the door open.

"I need to hear the bell if someone arrives," she said, looking uneasy as she faced Steph.

Steph motioned to her office chair. "It's probably more comfortable in the front office."

"That's okay." Emily lowered herself to the tile and sat. "Do you want to ask questions?" She looked to the ground. "I'd rather not go into details about me."

"No. That's fine." Steph sank into her desk chair and swiveled to face Emily. "I can imagine the memories still hurt."

Emily's hands knotted in her lap. "I'm ashamed. It happened before I knew Jesus, and now I can't believe I wanted to die."

Steph nodded, connecting with Emily's feelings—feelings that were so new to her. "Sometimes people are desperate."

She nodded, a thoughtful look covering her face. Emily brushed her long hair away from her face, her eyes direct. "How did he die?"

Steph told her the story, the way she'd been shocked, angry, confused, despondent and then numb. "But I pulled myself out of it and moved along." She paused, finding the right words. "Then for no reason the questions come back like a dart penetrating the pit of my stomach. Why? What did I do wrong? Could I have stopped him? Why didn't I see it?"

"Steph."

Her gentle voice whispered against Steph's ear, and she stopped. "Useless questions, right?"

Emily nodded. "Some people give warnings. They are depressed, withdrawn, give away their belongings. Usually those are the people who are crying for help. They don't really want to die, but they don't know what to do."

"Doug had been depressed, but he'd been that way for so long. He never gave anything away that I noticed."

"Taking your life is a desperate measure, but when someone is determined, nothing will stop him. It'll happen sooner or later."

She looked so matter of fact Steph couldn't respond. *Nothing will stop him.* "Nothing?"

Emily's eyes answered her question. "Steph, you can't read someone's mind, not someone who's determined. Don't beat yourself up."

But she had for so long. She lowered her eyes, and her watch came into view. Seven. Nick was coming at six-thirty. She was late.

Hal's welcome had been less than pleasant when Nick tried to carry on a conversation. He took an occasional furtive glance at his watch, then rose and paced along the wide window. Finally he stopped and rocked on his heels. "Do you think something's wrong?"

Hal clicked the TV remote to another station. "How should I know? The police haven't called."

Nick's muscles twitched in his arms. "You don't care much about your sister, do you?"

Hal arched his back and pulled himself into a sitting position. "What's that supposed to mean?"

The street was empty. Nick spun around. "Steph's usually not late. She might have—"

"Do you think you have a corner on being late?"

Hal's knifing comment pierced Nick and then twisted. But he was right. How often had he kept people waiting and sometimes never made it at all. It showed lack of respect, even self-centeredness. It had to stop. No more excuses. "You're right."

Nick sank into the chair and folded his hands in his lap. "Did you find a job?"

Hal's eyes widened.

"You haven't stopped by to fill out an application. I thought maybe you'd found something else."

A cocky look rose on his face. "Maybe I have."

His cell phone hummed in his pocket, sparing Nick from finding a civil answer. He flipped open the cover. "It's Steph."

Hal made a grunt sound as Nick pressed the phone to his ear.

"I'm on my way. I'm sorry, Nick. Time just whizzed past me."

With Hal eavesdropping, Nick couldn't say what he wanted to. "I'm glad you're okay. I was worried." But he'd wanted to tell her how he'd felt and what he'd learned. Instead she said goodbye.

When he flipped the phone closed, he slid it back in his pocket and decided to stare at the TV. It seemed easier. But the blat of the television faded as a love song merged into Nick's thoughts and the kiss. His pulse escalated. He'd wanted to open his heart that night, but it didn't happen, and since the wedding, he'd been tied up late at work. Brent's new order plus another large one, both a gift, had consumed his time with extra hours and work, but he welcomed it. He needed it to stay solvent. Yet he'd missed Steph.

On a positive note, her absence had given him time to think. When Nick was with her, he lost control of reality, and this time when he fell on his knee to ask a woman to marry him, he wanted to be confident. He wanted to feel the Lord at work in his life.

Places he needed to change or grow slithered through his mind—an endless list of ways in which he wanted to be a better person. His lateness had to stop, and his unwillingness to show emotions needed some work. Weeping publicly was not a prerequisite, but responding to someone's needs, even when his emotions tore him up inside, would make him a whole person. When Nick thought of this, his mother came to mind. Steph had helped him see that clearly.

Steph was good for him. She brought out the best and what wasn't best; he agreed it needed to be honed and shaped like the potter's clay.

At this moment and in this place, he believed Steph could be the one. But the word *could* gave him pause. A woman who shared his faith was the core of a good marriage. She'd begun to question and grow. All he needed was to be reassured that she had found the Lord. That would mean everything to him.

And for something this significant, he wasn't in a rush.

His eyes shifted from the blur of the television to Hal, sprawled on the sofa, reminding him of his own weakness when it came to his brother. Enabling. He and Steph were both guilty.

Steph pushed open the door, her eyes shifting from Nick to Hal and back again. She monitored her frustration with Hal by focusing on Nick. "Being late is the last thing I meant to do."

"Why apologize to him? He keeps you waiting all the time."

Nick's mouth opened then closed. He drew up his shoulders. "Hal's right. You have no need to apologize."

Her chest tightened. The sincerity in his face heartened her. When she shifted her gaze to Hal's dismayed expression, she had to stifle a laugh. Hal had met his match. He couldn't argue or make another comment because Nick had agreed. Smart move on Nick's part.

Letting the barbs fade, she touched Nick's arm. "Do you still want to go?"

His head drew back. "Sure." He faltered. "If you do."

"I'll be ready in a minute."

Steph certainly didn't want to stay at home with Hal.

In her bedroom, she slipped off her work clothes and looked into her closet. Nick wore jeans and a polo shirt. She loved seeing his tanned arms and his face the color of bronze. Taking his lead, she stepped into a pair of teal-colored capris and dropped a teal print knit top over her head. She freshened her makeup and ran a comb through her hair before grabbing her bag.

Nick had remained near the door while Hal pouted on the sofa. "Now that's a record." He motioned to her quick change.

"I'm anxious to enjoy the RiverWalk." And to get away from Hal. She stepped through the door, her heart heavy with what to do about her brother but buoyant to share the time with Nick.

Outside, he slid his arm around her shoulders and drew her close as he led her to the passenger side of his car. The comfort of his nearness eased the tension she'd felt with Hal.

Nick opened the sunroof as they drove, and the fresh air blew away the rest of her negative feelings. She hoped today they could really talk, alone and without interruption. But she feared when it came time, she wouldn't be able to tell him. Though she'd opened her heart to Julia, she had little to fear. The fragile woman made it easy. But with Nick? So much seemed to be at stake.

Nick exited I-375 on Jefferson Avenue, then found a spot in the Ford Underground Parking Garage. Steph exited the car before he could make it around to be a gentleman. Eager to get onto the plaza, they took the stairs rather than wait for an elevator, and when she stepped outside the lowering sun glinted off the Hart Plaza fountain—a strange-looking fixture like a doughnut on top of a bipod.

The gray, white and blue concrete captured the color of the sky—a pale blue dotted with wispy white clouds touched with gold. Nick tucked his fingers through hers as they crossed the plaza to the railing overlooking the Detroit River with the Ambassador Bridge stretching to Canada to her right and a glimpse of Belle Isle in the opposite direction.

In silence, they drew in the fresh air and the scenery, and Steph wafted in their closeness. Something new had happened, a sensation she couldn't explain and was afraid to understand. With Nick she'd found comfort and a kind of peace. Her mind thumped. Could it be God at work in her heart?

Without speaking, Nick slid his arm around her shoulders and turned her toward the Renaissance Center. A warm breeze ruffled her hair, and she'd noticed Nick looking at it. She'd kept it curled because he'd said how much he liked it. Straight took less time, but his compliment motivated her to do the extra work.

An empty bench appeared, and Nick drew her toward it. When she sat, her gaze drifted west to the Ambassador Bridge where the lowering sun touched the top of the steel towers that held the suspension cables. The sky had already begun to color with a sunset glow and splashes of gold sparkled on the ripples in the river.

"I'm disappointed in Hal."

Nick's voice cut through her solitude. His comment took her by surprise in this quiet spot. "So am I."

His brows knit as he searched her face. "Did he tell you?"

"Tell me what?" Concern rippled down her back.

"I told him to drop by and pick up an application. I may have an opening soon, and I would consider him if he's interested."

Her shoulders dropped, and the fresh breeze smelled stale. "He didn't tell me." She shifted on the bench to face him. "I'm sorry, Nick. He's… what? Disappointing? Lazy? Hopeless? Spoiled? Enabled?"

Nick brushed his fingers over her arms. "I didn't mean to upset you. I shouldn't have mentioned it."

"You did the right thing, but neither of us can change him. Hal has to do that himself. He's not willing to lift a finger to help himself, so why should you try?" Her stomach recoiled with the truth.

"Because I care." He tilted her chin toward him. "Not about Hal. About you." He shook his head. "It shows on your face. That confident attitude I loved, your sure smile, they've faded since he arrived. I know you feel responsible, but you shouldn't."

A muscle twitched in her cheek, and she released a ragged breath. "I know. I need to let it go and send him back to my dad's. But it's difficult."

Nick nodded. He understood, having to deal with his own issues. They both knew.

She stretched her legs out in front of her. "I wonder what Hal's living on?" For one thing, her. He had free room and board.

"By what he's living on, you mean money?"

She nodded. "Yes, money."

"Otherwise I'd say your sofa."

A laugh burst from her throat. "I couldn't have said it better myself."

Nick stood and reached for her hand. "Let's get cheerful again. We don't want the day to be a downer."

She grasped his hand and rose. The laugh had lifted some of her gloom, and hand in hand, they swung arms as they continued the walk. When they reached Rivard Plaza, Steph slipped her hand from his and ran ahead, stopping beside a charming carousel with bright blue and gilded reliefs circling a center mural of a lake and grass, trees and a blue sky the same color as it had been during the day.

Nick nestled behind her, his arms encasing her. He rested his chin on the top of her head. "Oh, to be young again."

She glanced at him over her head. "There's a little child in all of us."

He wiggled his eyebrows and gave a nod to the circling critters—fantasy fish, sea monsters, a stork, flying blue herons. "Want to?"

A grin tugged at her heart and then her mouth. "Sure."

Nick bought tickets, and when the carousel stopped and reloaded, they were side by side on what appeared to be two unusual fish Steph judged to be mermaids. Nick held her hand while they listened to the calliope sounds, but when they climbed off, Nick's smile had faded. "I have so much fun with you when we're not dealing with all these serious things."

Her heart squeezed, wishing she could bring back his smile.

"If we could get rid of all our baggage, think how great our time together could be."

She stopped, concern building in her mind. "Is this a goodbye?"

A look of surprise shot to his face. "No. Far from it."

"But, Nick, no one is ever free from problems. Even the greatest relationship has days that are heavy with trials. I think that's something the Bible tells us. This world isn't heaven. Not now, but it was supposed to be."

Beneath his worried look, she'd noticed the trace of something positive.

"What is it?" She paused along the walkway and leaned against the railing.

"You mentioned the Bible. That means a lot to me."

She opened her arms to him, and he drew closer as she wrapped her arms around his waist. "I know, and that's why I bought a Bible. What you believe and think means more than you know."

"You bought a Bible?" He leaned forward and gave her a quick kiss on the end of her nose. "You mean a lot to me, Steph. I see you making changes in your life and doing things that are positive. I need to do the same. I have so much to say, but I talk myself out of it so often."

The wind of fear spiraled in her mind. "Tell me."

He shifted position and joined her against the rail, his hand nestled in hers. "You've never asked me about other relationships I've had, and I've never talked about any."

Tension knotted along her spine. "I didn't think it was right to ask. We've had no commitment."

"It's not a criticism. Just a fact." He squeezed her hand. "I'm not good at talking about things, but I should because it's made an impact on my life. An impact I don't like."

A chill rolled her arms. "Were you married?"

"No." He rubbed his jaw, then dropped his arm. "But I was engaged. My folks thought she was great. So did I until things started to fall apart a few months before our wedding."

Steph sensed his guilt. "You ended the relationship?"

"No. Maybe." His frown deepened. "In a roundabout way."

Her eyebrows flew upward, and she hurried to control her reaction. "What do you mean?"

"She tugged off her ring and threw it at me, then said I didn't care enough about her. Everyone else came first."

Weight shifted on Steph's shoulders. "And that's why you think you caused the relationship to end?"

"I believed that for a long time."

I believed that. For so long she'd believed things that weren't true about herself.

"I judged that I couldn't be a good husband or father. Too many things distracted me. My business, my…"

He looked uneasy, and the weight settled back on her shoulders. If he were sharing his secrets, she needed to hear now before her heart became even more tangled in his life. "What else, Nick?"

"I did too much for other people." He shrugged. "You've seen me. I let my business distract me, Martin's always needing something, even you when we first met. I took on your fence problems with Martin even though you told me it wasn't my problem."

His head lowered, and he seemed to be studying the pattern in the walkway. "You were being kind. That's what you do."

"But Cara thought it took away from us, our time. I was late sometimes, and—" he lifted his head, an inquisitive look in his eyes "—you don't like that, either, do you?"

"No, and I don't think you like it."

"That's one of the things I wanted to tell you. When you were late today, I realized how self-centered and thoughtless that is." He held up his hand to stop her from commenting. "I'm not blaming you. Sometimes things happen and we're late, but I make a habit of it."

Steph nodded. Why lie to make him feel better? She had her own sins to deal with. "Nick, doesn't the Bible tell you to do things for others in the same way you'd like others to help you?"

He ran his fingers through his hair and nodded.

"Then you were doing what the Bible says to do."

"Yes, but if I turned my back on someone else in the process, I'm not sure that's what the Lord wants."

She slipped in front of him and rested her head on his chest. "Was Cara a believer?"

He shifted one arm around her and cupped her

head in his hand. "Her parents went to our church. She was raised a Christian. My parents thought our engagement was great."

Steph thought about what she'd said. "Non-believers can be good people, too. Helpful, kind, but someone born and raised in the faith should have understood. Did you ever think that it wasn't you at all?"

"That's what Martin said. Cara might have needed too much and maybe she did me a favor by walking out on me."

"Maybe she did." Though she agreed that Cara could easily have been at fault, Steph's mind drifted to her own frustration with Nick's lateness and Martin's demands that Nick met. He'd missed the wedding because of Martin. How would that affect someone committing a lifetime to Nick?

Steph remained silent. The question didn't need answering today. She lifted her eyes to the bridge, witnessing a gorgeous display of sunset on the horizon. She motioned to Nick.

He stood a moment, observing the nuances of change, the colors blending and flowing outward. Change of any kind began with nuances, gradually reaching a full metamorphosis. She'd wait and see Nick's transformation, and hopefully, he would notice hers.

"Look at the time."

Steph's head reared up, and she glanced at her watch. Nearly nine.

"You must be starving." He slipped his hand into hers. "Let's grab something to eat."

"We passed a couple of places down that way." She motioned toward Hart Plaza.

He clasped her hand in his. "I want to take you some place with good food and upbeat music."

Upbeat. That meant no more talk.

"Ever been to Hard Rock Cafe?"

"I've never been there." She realized he wanted to end the night on a cheerful note.

"They're headlining the Clay Adams Band, and I want you to hear them."

Steph nodded, not wanting to put a downer on his attempt to entertain her, but she'd hoped to talk. Nick had laid things on the line, and she needed to come out in the open, too.

Nick slowed, then stopped and dug into his pocket. He drew out his cell phone. "It's Martin." He dropped the phone into his pocket. "I'm not going to run his errands tonight."

Trying to control her surprise, Steph didn't say a word. The action meant a lot.

"Now it's a text message." Nick took her hand and started forward again, but he faltered, then dug into his pocket and looked at the screen. Concern grew on his face. "It's says 'Call me. 911.'"

What? 911? Her heart raced. "Then, call him."

He hit speed dial, his body tense. "Martin, what's wrong?"

Fear etch his face, and he continued. "Go home? Why? Is it Mother?"

Steph watched his face grow from fear to panic. "What is it, Nick?

"Fire?" He appeared frozen to the ground. "Are you sure, Martin?"

Fire? What was it? Steph's chest tightened.

"It's on the news. Is it bad?" He glanced at Steph, terror growing on his face. "I'll leave now." Nick closed the phone and dropped it in his pocket.

Steph grasped his arm. "What is it?"

"My apartment building. It's on fire."

Chapter Eleven

Flames licked skyward, and the smoke curled above him in the glow of the fire as Nick watched the building burn. He'd sent up a prayer, and so far his end of the complex had been spared. He knew smoke and water damage would make it unlivable, but his gratefulness grew as he watched the fire-fighters toil in the flames to save the building and those inside.

Steph leaned against him, his arm around her waist, and tears rolled down her cheeks. He gave her an extra squeeze, sorry she had to witness the fire but glad she was there. He hadn't felt so alone in a long time since meeting her, but watching the building burn sparked a new sadness. Like the parts of life, seeing them vanish and change to something unrecognizable was never easy. The apartment had been his step into freedom, and he hadn't budged.

One day he hoped other doors would open for another chapter in his life, one filled with love and companionship. And most of all, commitment.

"It's so sad." Steph's voice cut through the murmur of the crowd. "Did you realize I've never seen your apartment?"

He brushed her cheek with his finger. "It's nothing fancy. Nothing like your place." Sometimes he realized what little he had to offer any woman, but he had hope that one day things would be better for him financially.

She shook her head. "I wouldn't have that house without Doug, Nick. It wasn't my doing."

Her plaintive expression tore at his heart. "It was God's doing, Steph."

Her gorgeous eyes rimmed with tears gazed up at him. Her full lips flickered to a faint grin, so tempting he had to look away. "I should take you home. It's late."

"What about your things?"

"The police have my name and apartment number, and they said the fire's under control." He took a ragged breath. "I'll check in the morning to see when I can get in. I know I can't stay there."

A frown grew on her face. "Where will you go?"

The choice struck him. "The place I said I would never go."

She took a moment before she understood. "Martin's?"

He nodded. "And we're about the same size so I can borrow his clothes."

The frown vanished, and a grin worked on her lips. "Maybe this is God's doing. Did you ever think that this might be a time to reconcile?"

A chuckle rose in his throat. Would God really do that to him? "He's almighty and He might make it work, but I'm doubtful. What about the old saying that absence makes the heart grow fonder?"

She wrinkled her nose. "Don't believe it. Being face-to-face resolves issues. Absence just locks it away for a while."

He drew her closer in a hug, then took a last look at the apartment building, feeling a heavy pain in his chest. He pulled his eyes away and returned to the car and headed toward Martin's.

Nick checked his watch when he pulled into Steph's driveway. Two in the morning. "I'm so sorry this evening didn't go as planned."

She touched his face. "I agree we didn't plan this, Nick, but there's a purpose for everything. Know that something good will happen. I'm only sorry you have to deal with all the water damage."

Nick searched her serious eyes. "Did you realize you're using Scripture?"

She gazed at him, heavy-lidded, exhausted he

knew. "It makes sense. So has so much I've read. I'm grateful."

He stroked her cheek. "So am I."

Steph leaned closer and gave him a gentle kiss. When she drew back, she pressed her palm against his heart. "You don't have to walk me to the door. I'll see you tomorrow." She pushed the door handle and stepped out to the driveway. "Good night, Nick. I hope you rest well."

He did all he could do to jump from his seat and take her in his arms. "Until tomorrow."

She waved, climbed the porch steps and slipped inside. "Thank you, Lord." Though mentally exhausted, he sat a moment, watching her shadow against the drawn curtains. He released a lengthy breath before backing up and going inside to face Martin. Although they had their arguments, Nick knew Martin would take him in.

Putting his gear shift in Reverse, Nick pulled into his brother's driveway. When he stepped from the SUV, he realized how tired he was. As he moved toward the steps, Martin opened the door.

"I thought you'd call."

"Sorry, I didn't think of it. I spoke to the police—"

Concern etched Martin's face as he pushed open the screen door. "Is everything lost?"

Martin had actually worried about him. "No. My place has water and smoke damage, I'm sure but it's still standing. The firefighters had it under control when I left."

Martin opened his arms, and Nick stepped into his embrace. Being hugged by his brother felt strange but welcome. "Thanks for your concern and for calling me when you saw it on the news."

When Martin released him, he collapsed onto the sofa and leaned back, realizing his limbs were shaking. "It's just hitting me now."

"Coffee? It's fresh."

"Thanks. Maybe I will."

He started to rise, but Martin waved him back. "I'll get it."

The special attention from his brother was rare, but he appreciated it. His mind swam with things he would need to add to his busy time at work—filling out the insurance company forms, shopping for clothes and telling his mom. He hated to upset her.

He smelled the coffee before Martin carried it into the room. His stomach gnawed, but he knew he couldn't eat a thing. He grasped the cup Martin offered and took a sip. Black and hot.

Martin settled into the recliner and set his cup on the table beside him. "When it came on the news I prayed you weren't home. You can't believe my relief when I knew you weren't there. Where were you?"

"I took Steph to the RiverWalk at Hart Plaza. We were heading for Hard Rock Cafe when you called." He studied his brother, waiting for him to make a comment at the mention of Steph. He didn't. Nick's head whirred even more, wondering why.

Martin reached for his cup. "She sent me a card."

A card? "Steph sent you a card?"

He shielded his reaction by studying his coffee. "She told me how relieved she was to learn Suzette was okay." Martin finally lifted his head. "Under the circumstances, it was thoughtful."

"Very thoughtful." The news startled Nick, and it lifted Steph higher in his esteem…if he could lift her higher.

"That mutt of hers hasn't been too bad."

Nick monitored his tone. "Border collie."

He nodded. "Fred."

The compliment, and that's what it was, came out of nowhere. Nick had wondered if Martin could ever change, and today his hope grew a few inches more.

Martin tilted back in the recliner, his stocking feet rising in the air. Nick noticed a worn spot in one. His brother needed someone to care about him. A woman. They both did. Couples supported each other. They told him when they had spinach in their teeth or a hole in their sock. They leaned on each other and lifted each other up. Steph's tears let him know how much she cared.

"Do you have any plans until you can get back into your place? I hope you know you can stay here."

"Thanks. I thought I would if you don't mind."

"I'm your brother. You've done a lot for me, Nick, and I'm just beginning to realize that."

Whoa. Nick couldn't believe his ears, but he was grateful. Steph's observation jarred his thoughts. *Maybe this is God's doing. Did you ever think that this might be a time to reconcile?* Maybe it was and while he was at it, Nick decided to go for it all. No more belittling his business. He grinned, knowing soon Martin couldn't belittle it. In the past few days, sales were pouring in, and this year might be a banner year for profit. And he couldn't forget Suzette's obedience training.

But making changes went both ways, and Nick realized he needed some training, too. Being inconsiderate had to stop. No more being late. If he ever asked anyone to marry him again, he wanted to make sure he'd learned his lesson.

Steph's teary eyes hung in his mind. If anyone could train him, she could.

The sofa was empty.

Steph dropped her package and shoulder bag on a chair, then passed the guest room. The door was open, and Hal's clothes were still there. The realization left her with mixed emotions. She hung her head, cringing that she couldn't be more decisive. Somehow she needed to get through to her brother. He was too young to lead a wasted life, and that's exactly what he was doing.

She grabbed a glass from the cabinet and filled it with some iced tea, then returned to the living room. After picking up the package, she slipped into her recliner and leaned back. Nick had been on her mind all day. Since the fire, he'd only had time to call. One evening, he'd dropped in for a few minutes, but most of the time was filled with Hal's snide remarks. She had no idea what her brother's problem was, but it was clear he didn't like Nick for some reason.

Opening the parcel, she eyed the book on dealing with grieving after suicide. When Doug first died, she'd attended a couple of grief meetings, but they didn't address the kind of grief she struggled with. Most had lost husbands after many happy years of marriage or parents whom they loved but all from natural causes. The grief didn't seem to fit.

After her talk with Emily, she'd given much thought to her feelings, especially that the trauma of his death had surged over her like a tidal wave recently. The intensity occupied her thoughts and the old sense of hopelessness overwhelmed her.

The Bible had given her new ideas about life and

purpose, and so had Nick. She realized if she could understand her emotions, she could be on the road to being healthy again. She opened the book, scanning the preface. At the bookstore, she'd sat in a chair and read the opening before she bought the book.

So much fell into place, her feelings of anger and guilt, of being abandoned and being to blame. The points were all there. As she perused the chapters, one caught her attention. The message jarred her. She'd been given no clues that Doug had been that desperate. She'd already distanced herself from him when their relationship had begun to crumble. She'd tuned him out and had dealt with survival. Reading, she understood that marriages or relationships in trouble compounded the depth of grief. Not only had she dealt with the loss of their relationship but she had to accept that Doug's voluntary death left her with no opportunity to make their marriage better—no chance to forgive or to atone.

Tears blurred her eyes, and she lowered the book, wishing she'd purchased it years ago. Today she had a better grasp on her grief from Emily's comments, and she knew the book would strengthen her, too. Weeks ago, Steph had asked herself why now. Why had all these emotions come crashing down on her after four years and as strong as they were when it happened?

The question could end. She finally understood.

When Nick came into her world, she wanted to change and to look to the future, but she'd been so busy looking behind her that she couldn't see the future. With his first kiss, she continued to battle her heart, but the battle could end. Yes, she still had issues to resolve, but the one that drained her would end now.

The doorbell chimed, and Steph's pulse skipped. Hal had left his key somewhere. He was another issue that needed handling. She set the book on the lamp table and pulled open the door. Her pulse did more than skip. "Nick." Her heart smiled seeing him. "How are things?"

He stepped inside and drew her into his arms. "Okay. I still have some issues with the insurance company, but everything will be fine."

"And Martin? How are—"

"Better than I expected." He gave her a squeeze and shifted back. "He was very impressed that you sent him the card."

"I really meant it. Fred would have been heartbroken."

A grin broke on his tired face. "And you'll never believe it, but he agreed that Suzette needs obedience training."

The dark circles under his eyes attested to his stress. Even his tan seemed faded. She pressed her palm against his cheek. "That's great. I want to work with Fred a little more, too. I need to stop him from chasing squirrels."

Nick craned his neck as he looked past her. "Where is he?"

She chuckled. "In the back if you mean Fred. If you mean Hal, I have no idea."

His tired eyes widened. "Did Hal—"

"No. His clothes are still here." She motioned for him to sit while her mind dealt with a mix of emotions. She had no idea what to do for Hal.

Nick headed for the recliner. "I'm exhausted."

"You look it. You need to rest."

"I know." He drew up his shoulders, and as he did his focus landed on her book. He picked it up and turned it over to read the back cover blurb.

Steph wished she'd put it anywhere but where he would see it, but then maybe that was one of those things that happen for a reason. Rather than try to retrieve it, she sat on the sofa and curled her legs under her.

When he finished, he set it back on the table and looked at her. "Suicide?"

She nodded. "I've never told you how Doug died."

He flinched. "That's why you're reading the book?"

She looked away, getting her thoughts in order. "I've been trying to deal with this for years, but lately it's grown into a monster. I've been very confused."

His face grew attentive as Steph told him the confusions she'd felt in the past weeks since meeting him. "One thing I've learned recently is the Bible is filled with truth, and besides posing questions, it provides answers. After carrying this load with me since Doug took his own life, I didn't know how to let it go. When I read the verses that talked about Jesus carrying my burdens, I realized that he doesn't want to carry them if He has to drag me along with them."

A grin grew on Nick's face. "That's one way to look at it, and we're not really letting go when we hang on."

"That's what I've been thinking. So—" she gestured toward the book "—I realized I had to let it go, and I could only do that if I understood what I was carrying."

He flipped the footrest down and moved to sit beside her. "Once in a while I saw a look in your eyes that I didn't understand. You'd be smiling and lighthearted, then you'd withdraw. I thought it was something I'd done."

"The only thing you've done is make me happy, and make me see what I've been missing. I want to live again, Nick, but for so long, I've felt as if I missed something with Doug. I should have known and stopped him. We'd drifted far apart before the end. We didn't relate, and I thought it was something I'd done. He acted as if the cause was me, and I began to believe him. That meant I wasn't worthy to be part of anyone's life, and—"

"And you couldn't love again because you'd fail at it."

Her breath drained from her body. "Yes, how did you know?"

"Because I felt the same way."

She moved closer and slipped his hand in hers. "I didn't mean to burden you with this. You have too much on your mind."

"I'm glad we talked."

She rose and pulled him from the sofa. "I want you to go home and sleep." She guided him to the door, but Nick stopped and put his arm around her. "You have a lot of things on your mind, too. You are guiltless, and you need to know that. Pray about it, Steph."

"Do you think God would listen to me?"

"I'm not going to answer that. Read the Scriptures. Your answer is there."

He kissed the end of her nose, then lowered his lips to her mouth. The brief kiss touched her heart. "Sleep. Get some rest."

He gave her a wink and stepped outside.

She watched him go, feeling as if he'd been in her life forever.

Chapter Twelve

The dew glinted on the lawn, and Steph's sandals didn't protect her from the dampness. As she headed for Nick, Fred shot across the grass to rub noses with Suzette through the fence.

Nick waved, his hair tousled as if he'd just awakened. Seeing him there with the sun spreading highlights through his summer-tinted hair and his inviting smile made her feel complete. She'd given up on fighting her heart.

She grasped the fence. "How are things at the Davis household?"

Nick placed his hands over hers. "Unbelievable." He studied her a moment. "That's a good unbelievable."

"I'm glad." She saw the difference in his face; the strain had vanished. She'd feared it wouldn't happen, but she'd prayed, really prayed. It had felt strange but good.

"You may have been right."

Right? She tilted her head.

"About this being God's plan for reconciliation."

Her heartbeat did a double kick. "Really?" She saw in his eyes he meant it. "What happened?"

"You know the night of the fire Martin welcomed me to stay as long as I needed, although I don't think it will be more than a week or two. I talked to the insurance company and the manager of the apartment complex. They've already begun cleanup. The fire only damaged the far end of the building."

"That's great news." It was, but a hint of disappointment slithered to her heart. He'd be gone, and she loved his closeness.

"And, believe it or not, Martin had no complaints when I asked to borrow some of his clothes."

"Another first?" His expression caused her to grin.

"Yep, but I did pick up a few things." He pointed to his pullover shirt and jeans.

"They look good." *Good* wasn't the word. Appealing. Gorgeous. Handsome.

"And one more thing."

A grin stole to his face.

"Martin admitted how much I do for him and his ungratefulness."

"Nick, that's amazing." Her chest tightened. "Did I tell you I prayed for you and Martin?"

His eyes searched hers. "Thank you, and God heard your prayers. Do you see how prayer works?"

"Not a coincidence? That's what I always thought when I wished for something and it finally happened."

"Nothing happens without God's knowledge. Even evil. We learn from bad things. We grow closer to Him." He curled his hand beneath hers and drew them to his chest. "It's hard for nonbelievers to understand. They think we're deluded and gullible, but if we look for the positive, we can find it. And one day, when we see Him—"

"Face-to-face, we'll understand." She'd heard Molly say that, but then it had no meaning. Today it did.

He lifted her hands to his mouth and kissed them. "He mentioned getting a dog walker for Suzette. Someone who'll come in and take her for a walk, play with her a little during the day."

The dog recognized her name and pranced to Nick's side with Fred following. Nick released her hands and reached down to scratch Suzette's head.

"I know someone who is a dog sitter." She motioned in the direction of Time for Paws. "She works at the shelter part time. I can ask if she has time for another customer."

"You can trust her?"

"Yes. She's very conscientious." She pictured Emily's love of dogs and her honesty.

"Martin admitted he doesn't spend enough time with Suzette." He drew in a lengthy breath. "But I don't know if that will change. He's work-driven." He flicked his shoulder. "We'll see." He gave the dog another pat, but a squirrel chittering in the trees captured her attention along with Fred's. They bounded away, tails alert as they faced their adversary.

Adversary. Steph lowered her head, facing her latest concern. Telling Nick could cause another problem, but she needed someone's advice.

His brows knit. "What's wrong?"

"Speaking of trust." She drew up her shoulders. "I have another problem. One I dread dealing with."

He scowled and pointed to his chest.

"Not you." She wanted to hug him because he looked so dismayed. "The day of the wedding I noticed some twenties missing from my wallet. I'd been shopping, and I tried to remember if I'd paid cash and forgotten, so I let it go. A couple days ago the same thing happened, and Wednesday when I bought that book, money was missing from my purse. This time I knew it was really missing, because I'd been more cautious and paid attention to what I had in my wallet."

Nick pressed his lips together as if he didn't want to comment.

Lowering her head, she struggled to admit whom she suspected. "It's Hal. That's the only thing that makes sense." Despair rose to her throat, and she choked. "I can't believe it."

Nick reached across the chain links and stroked her arm. "That's not good, Steph."

"I know. I have to talk with him, and I know he'll deny it." Imagining the confrontation roiled in the pit of her stomach. "I don't know what to do."

"What about your dad? Can you call him? He may have had the same problem."

Steph could see Nick's mind clicking. "I should. Then I'll know if it's a continuing problem or something new."

"I should be glad he never followed up on the job application." The frown hadn't left Nick's face. "But you can't live this way. You know that."

The truth felt like a boulder pressing on her heart. "You're right. I'll let you know what my dad says."

"Then you'll have some ammunition. And, Steph?"

Hearing her name, she looked up.

"You know prayer works." A look of concern grew on his face.

"It does." How easy it was to admit it surprised Steph.

"Let's do something tonight." Nick's face brightened. "Anything. You need to get away from here today."

"I'd love it." She wanted to run as far as she could from her problems, and she knew they would just follow her until she dealt with them.

"I'll talk with you later." He backed away and clapped for Suzette to follow with no success. Instead, he grasped her collar and led her to the back door.

Fred whimpered while Steph watched them go inside. She and Fred, two of a kind. "Come." She turned toward the dog, but he remained pressed against the face. Another whimper alerted her.

"Fred?"

He tried to move but he seemed to be caught.

Steph hurried to the dog's side and crouched beside him, realizing his ID tag had hooked to the fence. She wiggled the metal, finally pulling the tag from Fred's collar. He sprang away, and she rose, holding the tag. She dropped it into her pants pocket to repair inside.

"Fred, you and I are both hooked, aren't we?" She clapped her hands, and this time Fred followed her to the patio. When they entered the kitchen, Steph knew she had a grin on her face. It felt good.

Steph sat in her bedroom, feeling captive. She and Nick had enjoyed the evening, but the telephone call to her father kept repeating in her ears. Yes, Hal stole money. He'd even hocked a couple of items from the house. "I've had enough of him," her dad had said, his voice sounding tired. She needed to visit him. It had been too long.

When she talked it over with Nick, he agreed with her. Though it would be difficult, she had to confront Hal and send him packing. When Steph thought back, Hal had caused her to have doubts about Nick. His continual comments about Nick's lateness and his wanting something from her had messed with her mind until she put things in perspective. She knew Nick better than Hal.

Last night when she returned home, she'd hoped for enough courage to talk with Hal, but he came in after she did and smelled of alcohol. That wasn't the time to talk, but this morning would be. She couldn't let it drag on.

She made her way to the kitchen to fortify her courage with a cup of coffee. While starting the pot, she heard Hal's snores coming from his room. She sank onto a chair and lowered her head.

Why couldn't they have a loving brother-sister relationship? Nick and Martin squabbled occasionally, but when things were tough, they were there for each other. She tried to think back to her childhood. Her role model had been her mother, and though Steph had more backbone than her mother, she had always tried to be kind as her mother had been. Hal had their dad as his role model, a poor example. Could she blame it on that? People could grab their necks by the collar and lift themselves up and find strength deep inside their own abilities and experience. Failure wasn't genetic.

At this moment, Steph wished she could talk with Nick, but she knew he'd gone to church. Church. He'd invited her once, but she hadn't been ready. The idea of walking into a place she'd never related to most of her life made her uneasy. Yet the past couple of weeks she'd altered her attitude. If he asked today, she would be tempted to go.

It wasn't as if that's where God lived and she would have to see Him face-to-face. She knew better than that. Jesus stood beside each Christian every day. He walked with them and listened. Steph gazed around the room, wishing she could see His shadow or hear His footsteps, but it had to do with trust and faith. Most of life needed the same qualities. What was a marriage without trust? What was purpose and the future without faith?

She had finally caught on.

Fred let out a bark and skidded across the tile floor. He pressed his nose against the patio door. A squirrel or Suzette. Steph knew the routine. "Fred. No."

He glanced at her, his tail wagging, but his barking continued. Her second "no" drew him from the doorway to his bowl.

Steph rose and poured dog food into his dish and refreshed his water. Before she sat down, Hal wandered into the room in a T-shirt and jogging pants. "Can you keep that dog quiet?"

Tension charged up her spine. "It's ten-fifteen. The rest of the world is up, Hal."

He ignored her and poured a cup of coffee before sticking his nose into the refrigerator. "What's for breakfast?"

"Anything you'd like to make." Her heart pounded, knowing what she had to do.

He glanced at her over the door. "You're kidding, right?"

"No, I'm not." She drew in a ragged breath. "Would you sit for a minute?"

"Why?" He gave her a cranky look.

"Because I asked." She motioned toward a chair.

He grasped his cup and shuffled to the table, then pulled out a seat and sat. After a swig of coffee, he peered at her with his okay-what-do-you-want look.

"I talked to Dad this morning."

He shrugged. "So?"

Blood throbbed in her temples. "I asked him

if you'd ever stolen money from him." She held her breath.

His smug look vanished until he managed to recover. "I never stole money from him. I borrowed it."

"Without asking."

Hal didn't respond. Instead he stood and grabbed his cup. "I'm not going to sit here and listen to—"

"That's right." Her chest ached with the panic.

He did a double take, then recovered again. "Good."

"Hal, I mean, you're leaving." She clenched her trembling hands.

He spun around. "Leaving? Where'll I go?"

The first words that fell in her mind weren't what God would have her say. She struggled to find words. "I don't know, but you're leaving here." A sense of determination lifted her. "If I were you, I'd go back to South Carolina where you have friends and more opportunity for work."

"I'm not living with Dad." He looked like a pouting child.

"Dad won't take you back. You need to grow up. You're thirty-two and—"

"Thirty-three."

She rolled her eyes. He missed the point. "That's even worse. You need to stop drinking and whatever else you're doing with your money and make a useful life for yourself. Life's nothing without purpose and right now, you—"

"The boyfriend told you to kick me out, didn't he?"

"You're wrong, Hal." Anger flashed through her. She wanted to deny Nick was her boyfriend, but what was the point. He'd given her more than friendship and kindness. He'd helped her realize how much she needed the Lord. "You can blame him if it makes you feel better."

Hal's smirk grated on her.

Courage spurred her on. "Actually your barbs and insults worked the opposite. The more you criticized, the more I realized what a gem he is. The man is honest, kind, thoughtful and—"

"Late." He chuckled.

"And late sometimes, but if that's his biggest flaw, I can live with it."

"Now I get it, he wants to move in so he can get a little—"

Her body sparked with fire, and she wanted to smack him. "That's your life, brother. I don't live with men. I don't give myself without marriage. That's the last thought on my mind."

"Come on. Don't play coy. You've been married. What are you saving—"

She held up her hand to stop him. "Not in my house. I'm not lowering myself to carry on this conversation. I'll give you today to find a place to stay or get yourself packed, but tomorrow when I come home from work, you'll be gone." She stood and shoved her chair under the table. "This isn't the kind of relationship I want with you, Hal. Not at all. But it's come to this and I'm not changing my mind. Tomorrow you're gone."

She didn't wait for a response.

Nick placed his hand over his mother's. "You're not worried are you? Everything's fine, and I'll be back in my apartment in a couple weeks."

"I praise the Lord you weren't home." Her translucent skin was mottled with a pink flush.

"See, Mom? I put color in your cheeks." His mother's speech had reverted nearly back to normal, and he thanked God for the blessing.

She gave him a playful swipe. "I'm much better. Much."

"I see that, and I'm grateful. Soon you can get back to your own place."

A sweet smile lifted her cheeks. "Funny. I hated moving to an assisted-living residence, and now I look forward to going back."

He chuckled. "Told you." He searched her eyes, hoping she would be glad with his next news. Nick drew closer, his blood pumping through his veins. "You like Steph, don't you?"

She gave him a questioning look. "You know I do."

"Did you know she wasn't a Christian?"

She gave a faint nod. "But I'm not worried about that."

"You're not?"

"She's curious and open, Nick. She's ready. I can sense the spirit sneaking in the crevices of her heart. I know she'll be a believer."

His shoulders relaxed, and a chuckle escaped him. "A mother's intuition."

"That and prayer."

His heart lifted seeing his mother's spirit and confidence. "You're right. I'm watching her grow every day, and you know it's important to me not only because I want everyone to believe, but—"

She touched his hand. "Because you're falling in love with her."

"You knew." His pulse escalated.

"Mothers always know. I'm happy for you. Life wasn't meant to be alone. Everyone needs a special someone, and I think you've found yours."

"If she feels the same." Though he wanted it to be true, the possibility of her feeling differently shook his confidence.

"Wait. You'll see."

Her tender smile refreshed his courage. "I won't rush into anything, but mothers are always right." He chuckled. "Isn't that what you've always told me?"

"Yes, and—"

Nick cell phone jarred her comment. He flipped the lid. "It's Steph." A smile flew to his lips just reading her name, but when he heard her voice it faded.

"Nick, I came home and Fred's gone."

"Fred? Don't you mean Hal?"

"Yes, he's gone, too, but Fred's missing." Her last word sank beneath her sobs.

Missing. Nick's heart thwacked against his chest. "Hang on, Steph. I'll be there. He's got to be nearby. I'm sure he didn't run away."

Hal. That's the only thought that struck his mind.

Chapter Thirteen

As soon as Nick walked in, tears poured from Steph's eyes, and her sobs distorted her words. "I've called everywhere. The police. The dog pound. I even called Time for Paws, hoping he found his way there."

Nick's vision blurred, picturing Fred wandering alone somewhere. "You didn't take him with you today?"

She used her fingers to dab at her eyes. "I took in two new dogs, so I left him home. He gets a little jealous." She shrugged. "You know."

He did. He pulled his handkerchief from his pocket and wiped the tears from her cheeks, then handed it to her. "Fred's smart. He'll find his way back."

"But why did he go?" She sniveled again. "It doesn't make sense."

His mind popped. "Fred has an ID tag, Steph. Someone will call you."

ID tag. Her heart sank to the pit of her stomach. "He did." The weight of stupidity brought tears to her eyes. "I think it's still in the pocket of my pants." She told him about the day the tag had caught on the fence. "It has his name and my cell-phone number." She brushed away her tears. "A lot of good it does me now."

Nick shook his head. "That's a bad break."

She nodded, then motioned toward the side of the house. "The gate was open, too. I never leave the gate open."

Nick fought to keep his thoughts covered. "I'm sure it was an accident."

She sank into an easy chair. "Hal's gone. Not even a note." She lowered her head. "Last night I told him I wanted him out by today."

Nick knelt beside her and clasped her hand. "I'm sorry about Hal's problems, Steph, but at least he did what you asked." His heart broke as he looked into her eyes.

Her head jerked upward as if yanked by a pulley. "Nick, you don't think—" she shook her head "—no. Hal wouldn't do that." Her eyes grew distant for a moment. "You don't think he would take Fred, do you? Just to get even?"

He had thought that, but he stifled the words. "Get

even for what? You did everything for him. Cooked his meals, let him stay here and encouraged him."

"And you offered him the chance for a job."

Her head fell against the chair back. "He was drinking last night." Her neck dropped forward. "And on my money. The bills he stole from my wallet. My own brother."

Nick realized that Martin wasn't so bad after all. At least he was honest. Too honest sometimes. Nick caressed Steph's hand, his mind spinning with what to do. How could he help? What if Hal did take the dog? He could drop him off anywhere, and the dog could get… No. Stop thinking that way.

Steph slipped her hands from his. "I can't just sit here. I need to do something." She grasped the chair arms and pulled herself up.

Nick scooted on his knees to move out of her way. "Let's make posters."

She spun around. "Yes." She snapped her fingers. "A photograph. I have some." She darted to the computer, her fingers flying over the keys.

Nick watched her, amazed at her organization. Having a purpose, her tears vanished. She sat with her face pointed at the monitor, clicking on photographs.

"Steph, what can I do to help?"

Her arm swung like a mad woman, motioning to storage trays beside her computer. "There's a pad of paper." Instead of waiting for him, she grabbed the pad and tossed it at Nick.

He caught it, ripping the top sheet.

"Jot down the information I'll need on the poster. I don't want to forget anything."

He kept his distance, wondering what she might throw next, yet admiring her determination.

In twenty minutes, Steph had a stack of golden-rod-colored posters clutched in her hand.

"Ready?" His eyes had opened as wide as grape-fruit watching her work.

She halted, as if she'd awakened from a deep sleep. "Thank you." She touched his cheek, then raised on tiptoes to kiss his lips.

Nick drew her closer, relieved to have Steph back in the real world, and while he held her in his arms, he prayed Fred would be back, too. He missed the crazy dog already.

Steph pulled into her driveway and sat a moment, finding the courage to go inside. Nearly two weeks had passed with no sign of Fred, and her heart ached when she stepped into the house without his greeting. She'd cried herself to sleep more nights than not. If she only knew what had happened, she'd at least have closure.

Closure? Closure wasn't what she wanted. Steph wanted a happy ending. Every day, she looked out the front window waiting for him to come to the door or bark or maybe a car would pull up in answer to her posters all over the neighborhood. She'd go out, and Fred would be in the backseat.

Even Nick had spent hours with her in the evenings, driving through the neighborhood putting up the posters, and asking people along the way if they'd seen a border collie. She carried his photograph and extra posters just in case. Tears rolled down her cheeks as she turned off the ignition and stepped onto the driveway. Since Fred had gone she couldn't face the backyard or her stupidity.

She slammed the door and headed to the street for her mail. As she stepped between the houses, Martin stood at his mailbox. She hesitated, not able to bare his snide comments. Before she could move back, he saw her and waved. Trying to be genial, she waved back, then faltered when he came across the grass.

"I'm sorry to hear about Fred."

Sorry? Steph bit her tongue to keep her sarcastic remarks at bay. "Thank you."

His eyes studied hers as if he wanted to say more or expected her to say something else. They faced each other in silence.

Martin dug his hands into his pockets. "I know I haven't been very friendly, but I would neve wish anyone to lose their pet. I know how much he meant to you."

The kindness was too much for her. Tears bubbled along her lower lashes, and she didn't have the strength to wipe them away. "It's been hard. I can't imagine Fred running away." She gestured toward the backyard. "Someone left the gate open." Hal's image pierced her mind.

"I thought about that when Nick told me." He motioned to the house on the other side of hers. "The boy who lives there came into your yard around that time—I think about then—to retrieve a ball."

"Next door?"

"I saw him and watched because I wondered what he was doing. Fred was outside. I'd heard him barking at a squirrel again." He shook his head. "He and Suzette are two of a kind when it comes to those critters."

"Squirrels?" She hadn't thought of that. "Did you notice the gate? Did he leave it open?"

"I'm not certain, but he had a friend over, I think. The kid was hanging over the fence pointing to where the ball had gone. When I saw what they were doing, I walked away."

"Thanks for telling me, Martin." Hal? Could she be wrong? "That means a lot to me."

He drew his hand from his pocket and gave her shoulder a pat. "I hope you find him."

"Me, too, and thanks again."

He took a step backward, looking more awkward then she could ever imagine Martin looking. She thought about Suzette's horrible mishap as she pulled her mail from the box, wondering if that had caused Martin's change in attitude. As Steph headed up the driveway, a car sounded behind her and she turned. Nick parked behind her and slipped out. "Any news?"

She shook her head, then told him about Martin's visit and what he'd said about the neighbor boy. "I don't know what to think."

He slid his arm around her and gave her a hug, and again she fought her tears.

"Come in." She beckoned him to follow, and inside she dropped her handbag on a chair and looked at him. "How are you doing?"

"Good. I can check the apartment tonight. If everything's okay, I can move back this weekend." He sent her a grin. "If you come with me, you can see my place."

She managed a grin. "You don't have an ulterior motive, do you?"

"Me?" He gave her a wink. "I would never ask you to help me put the place back together."

"Sure." She waved him away and headed into the kitchen. "I'm going to call my dad. I've been blaming Hal for Fred's absence, and now I wonder after hearing what Martin said."

"That's a good idea." He pulled out a chair and straddled it.

Before Steph lifted the phone, she spotted the voice-mail button blinking. She pressed the retrieval button and listened, and when she heard the women's voice her heart rose to her throat. "Listen to this." She started the message again.

"This is Marlene Landing. I saw a poster about your missing dog. A few days ago, I saw him wandering along a side street near my home and took him in, but he jumped the fence before I could do anything. Please call me."

Steph's heart dropped. "Fred got away again." Her hands shook as she jotted down the woman's telephone number. "If that's so, then Hal didn't take him."

"Maybe it wasn't Fred, Steph. Border collies can look alike."

"I know, but—" she pressed her fist against her churning stomach "—I'll call Dad first, then I'll call her."

She punched her father's number, then looked at Nick's serious face. He cared as much as she did. It made her feel twice as bad. The phone rang, and when her father picked up, she posed the question.

"No?" She shook her head and covered the phone. "No dog." She pulled her hand away. "Dad, is he staying with you?"

She looked at Nick and shook her head again. "Good for you. So what happened?"

Nick rose and moved beside her, his arm around her shoulders as she listened to her father's story, and when she hung up, she moved into Nick's embrace. "Hal has a job. He found a studio apartment. Dad wouldn't let him stay."

"Good for your dad and for you. That's what he needed."

"All these years." She lowered his head to Nick's chest and stood a moment, getting a grip on her emotions and reviewing all that she'd learned.

Nick's arms held her close, giving her comfort. She felt ready to give herself over to falling in love, and she hoped Nick felt the same. Between the fire and Fred, everything else had taken a backseat.

When her pulse had slowed, she drew her head up and looked at him. "I'll call that woman, but it seems useless."

"But you'll know where Fred has been, and we could look around there. Maybe put up some more posters."

"But I thought you wanted to go to the apartment today."

He gave her a squeeze. "We can do that, too." He tipped her chin upward and kissed her on the tip of the nose. "You need to get out of this house."

The sorrow washed over her again. "I have

Fred's things in a pile in the garage, and I know I should throw them away. Every time I look at them I…" She couldn't say the words without sobbing.

Nick didn't speak. He held her close, and her mind filled with how life had chanced since he'd darted into her life to rescue her. But the rescue had gone beyond this life; eternity waited for her as her faith grew. He'd provided her with answers and most of all his gentle compassion.

"It's a nice apartment, Nick." Steph pivoted as she looked at the open floor plan. "It looks roomy."

"But not as roomy as your place, and no pets here." He winced, obviously sorry that he reminded her of Fred again.

"It's okay." She put his hand in hers and kissed his knuckles. "We put more posters now in the new area. Just maybe…"

He drew her into his arms and searched her face. "I know it's been horrible for you, because I'm sick about it, and he wasn't my dog. But don't give up. Dogs have an instinct."

"It's been two weeks. It's time to give up." She drew away, unable to look at his sad eyes. She'd learned to read so much in their depths. She slapped her hands together, hoping to chase away their sadness. "What can I do to help?"

"I need to look around first, and if everything

seems good, then I'll put everything back. All my clothing and linens—everything—had to be cleaned from smoke damage. Even my dishes and pans." He chuckled. "I do own a few dishes even though I don't cook much."

She grinned and followed him into the kitchen area. Everything gleamed and looked spotless compared to her kitchen.

"I bet you're hungry. I am." He tugged his cell phone from his pocket. "I'll order a pizza." He pushed a button and grinned. "I have it on speed dial."

She couldn't help but laugh.

After he made the call, Nick pulled two soft drinks from his refrigerator and snapped the tops. He handed her one. "I'd offer you a glass, but they're still in boxes."

"This is fine." Her mouth had dried, thinking of the things she'd like to say to him. She took a sip and followed him as he beckoned her into the living area.

Nick motioned for her to sit while he chose his recliner. "It's been a difficult couple of weeks, I know."

"Yes, but I've also had time to think." She gathered her thoughts, wanting to open her heart and prayed he could do the same. "We've both had a bad time. You with the fire, but it all turned out okay, and me…" The words wouldn't come.

He nodded. "Be positive. I know it seems hopeless, but think of Lassie."

Lassie. She laughed.

Nick waved away his words, laughing with her. "Forget it. Just think positive."

"You've helped me do that, and I'm so grateful, Nick. So much of my life has…" She swallowed, longing to speak from her heart. "My life has been lonely. After Doug's suicide, I felt responsible. When I saw how unhappy he seemed, I tried to talk with him, but he turned the conversation around to me. I needed to get a life. He had one. I needed to be more understanding. I needed to see a shrink. I drove him crazy."

"Steph. You knew better." Nick's frown deepened.

"I did at first, but the worse things became, the more I began to doubt myself. I began to believe that I wasn't a good wife. I didn't meet my husband's needs. Our finances seemed tight at times. Doug made excellent money, but we never seemed to have it. He paid the bills so I didn't know what was happening." The weight of the memories pressed against her.

Nick lowered his elbows to his knees and folded his hands between his legs, a gloomy look etching his face. "I'm sorry you had to go through this."

She shrugged. "Maybe it made me stronger. Now that I've met you, I understand that my relationship with Doug wasn't typical. He must have had problems before I met him, and I didn't see it." She lowered her feet to the floor. "I had nothing to compare it to. My mom led a lonely life, too. She and my dad weren't partners. They seemed to just live in the same house. Do you know what I mean?"

He nodded, but she could tell he couldn't comprehend what she'd said.

"In the book I'm reading, I learned that sometimes years later people who've lost loved ones to suicide—the book calls us survivors—have upsurges of grief even though they'd thought they had healed."

Nick moved beside her. "Why?" He slipped his hand in hers.

"Something triggers it. An old song, a photograph, a souvenir from the past. It can be anything." She couldn't look at him, afraid he'd ask her more.

"What was it with you? Do you know?"

She felt her heart slip to her stomach. How could she tell him without setting herself up for hurt. "This is hard for me, Nick."

He cradled her hand in his. "I need to understand so I can help you."

She looked past him, searching for a simple way to say it. How could she say "because I fell in love with you"? "You opened my eyes to what a relationship should be. That was the first thing. We talked openly. We laughed. We enjoyed the dogs. Simple things."

"And then?"

"Then I realized that if I ever wanted a serious relationship with anyone, I wasn't capable. I wasn't worthy."

Nick drew her in his arms and held her tight. "You are so worthy. Worthier than anyone I know." He drew back and captured her gaze. "Do you know how much you mean to me?"

"You enjoy my company." Her pulse raced looking in his eyes.

"Enjoy? I love your company. I miss you when we're not together. I think about you all the time."

She closed her eyes, drinking in his sentiment.

"I think of you all the time." She raised her hands and cupped his face in her palms. "You helped me find the Lord. Molly had worked on me for years, but meeting you and your mom finished Molly's job. Now it makes sense and my faith is growing." She swallowed. "But I still don't understand why God cares about me. I denied him for so long."

"Steph. Steph. Have you read any verses about the Good Shepherd?"

She'd read so much, the Bible and the book on suicide, but she was blank. "I've heard Jesus called the Good Shepherd."

Nick's eyes shone. "One of Jesus' parables was

about a shepherd who owned a hundred sheep, and one strayed away. He left the ninety-nine alone to search for one sheep. When he found it, he carried it over his shoulders and returned it to the herd, rejoicing that he'd found his lost sheep." Expectation grew on his face as he looked at her and waited.

"I'm a lost sheep?"

"You were, but He found you and brought you back to the fold. You're a child of God, Steph, no matter what you thought of Him. He was your father all along and He loved you. That's why He cares, and that's why He forgives."

Tears bubbled in her eyes and rolled down her cheeks. The parable explained what she hadn't been able to grasp, and Nick's love of God shown through.

He brushed away her tears but didn't speak.

"Thank you. You've given me so much. You make me feel whole."

He drew her into his arms, his lips touching hers before he spoke. "And you've opened windows for me. Between you and Martin, I realize that God hadn't planned for Cara and I to be married. We weren't soul mates, and I should be grateful to her for returning the ring. She needed more than I could give, but that doesn't make me wrong. Just wrong for her."

"It's funny how we don't realize things when they happen." The thought had been niggling at her since she'd realized how much Nick meant to her. Her throat tightened. "It's hard to talk about this but when I found Doug, I—"

"Steph." He grasped her shoulders and looked into her eyes. "You found him?"

The vision flooded her mind—the rope, the gaseous smell. She nodded. "At home."

"Oh, my love." His voice quaked. "By yourself?" His question was a whisper.

"When I opened the garage door and saw him hanging there with the car motor running."

"No." He drew her into his arms, his body shaking with her admission. "Horrible. Appalling."

"Like the last lash against me. The final chance to wound me." Her voice shook as she spoke. Other than the police, she hadn't told the full story. She'd kept it, feeling degraded by Doug's hostility.

"And you've lived there? You see that garage every day?" His voice whispered in her ears. "You need to move away from there, Steph. You'll never be free of it if you don't."

She drew back. "I try not to think about it, but I always did…that is until a month ago." She gazed into his eyes wondering if he would remember.

"A month ago." His eyes narrowed, and he looked away, his frown deepening. Then as if the sun rose on a cloudy day, he returned her gaze. "We kissed for the first time in the garage."

She nodded. "That's my memory now."

He drew her forward again. "Steph, I'll kiss you in every room in the house if I can make everything better."

Her heart sang. "Enough sad talk. Let's put things away and be happy."

Nick leaned forward and pressed his mouth to hers as the doorbell rang. He drew back. "Stay right where you are. I'll be back." He rose and dug his hand into his pocket. "It's the pizza." Shrugging, he grinned and hurried to the door.

Chapter Fourteen

Nick packed his belongings in the duffel bag and carried the rest to his SUV on a hanger. Though he'd dreaded the time with Martin, the two weeks hadn't been so bad. He loaded the car and walked back inside.

Martin leaned against the archway with a look on his face that confused Nick. "I'm sure you're happy to see me go."

Nick adjusted his shoulder. "Not really. I enjoyed having someone to talk with."

The sound of Martin's voice put Nick on edge. Martin didn't give compliments and sound sappy, but he did today.

Martin took a step forward. "Do you have a few minutes?"

"Sure." He settled on a chair, wondering if Martin would make another job offer.

"I've been thinking a lot lately, Nick."

His serious voice added to Nick's edginess. "What is it?"

"Perceptions."

Perceptions. Nick waited.

"I've been unpleasant for a long time. It took a while for me to realize it, and I want to thank you for helping me face the truth."

Nick struggled to keep his eyebrows from shooting up. "I haven't done anything."

"You have. Maybe without knowing it." He wandered across the room and slipped into a chair. "I've had to face some things." Martin squirmed in his chair. "I've been jealous of you for years. I didn't realize that was the problem, but that's it."

Nick bolted upright, his palm smacking his chest. "Jealous? Of me?"

"You handle things with honesty, Nick. You've forced me to do the same. I wanted your business to fail to prove to myself that I was worth as much—maybe more—than you. I was happy when Cara walked out on you, because my marriage was such a mess."

Nick's head spun, startled at Martin's admission but more so at the pain he saw in his brother's face.

"You've been my scapegoat for all the inferior feelings I've had, but the other day when we talked, I began to realize you were right. I didn't see things clearly. I was the one pushing me. Mom and Dad were proud of whatever I did. Yes, they expected me to do well, because I always did. I couldn't handle my failures. My marriage was one of them." He closed his eyes, then opened them. "I cause myself most of my grief."

Nick found his voice. "I can't believe you were jealous. I always admired your abilities. You were a better student than I was. Your business has grown and prospered. I don't see how you would see anything in me to cause you to be jealous."

"Because you're a good person. You care about people."

Nick held up his hand.

"I know you had a problem with Mom, but I understood that. You've always been too sensitive, and you and Mom had special connection. You were her baby. Probably always will be."

Nick chuckled. "She's a great mom, and it's such a relief to know she'll be going back to her place soon."

Martin nodded. "Anyway, I want to apologize for belittling you to try to make myself feel better, and I hope you can forgive me."

"Forgive you? There's nothing to forgive." He stepped forward and embraced his brother. Though the affection felt strange, it felt good. "Thanks for being open."

Martin stepped back. "Here's one more thing."

Now for the truth. Nick held his breath.

"I'd like you to take Suzette."

The air shot from his lungs. "Me? Take Suzette? What are you talking about?"

"You spend more time with her than I do, and you said you'd get her obedience training. You know I won't."

Nick's mind spun. Suzette. He loved the dog. "I can't have a dog at the apartment, Martin, so I can't accept your offer." He pictured Suzette being his own. "As much as I'd like to take her."

"She can stay here. Your business is growing, and you'll have a house soon." He tilted his head toward Steph's. "Anyway, I'm hearing wedding bells, and the bride has a house."

Heat rose up Nick's neck. "Am I that transparent?"

"It's that face of yours. It talks louder than you do."

Nick wondered how much Steph had read. "Are you sure about Suzette?"

His face darkened, and Nick suspected he was thinking of Fred as Nick did so often. "Positive. Suzette might fill the empty space just a little."

Nick doubted that but maybe in time. Steph's sad face lingered on his mind, and it broke his heart. He would do anything to make her feel better, but he knew it was in God's hands. "It's a deal." He extended his hand, and Martin shook it.

Martin drew up his shoulders. "One day, maybe I'll try again, and I know Suzette is in good hands."

"She will be, Martin."

As he headed outside, Nick hoped Suzette would be in four good hands instead of two. He darted across the front lawn, tapped on Steph's door and opened it.

She gave him a wide-eyed look, motioning him to come in. The phone was clasped to her ear, and as he neared, he saw tears rolling down her cheeks but excitement in her voice.

"You're kidding? Really? I can't believe this."

Nick moved closer, anxiety building as he listened.

"Thank you. Thank you."

She dropped the phone, but instead of saying anything, she broke into a sob.

Nick clasped her shoulders. "What's wrong?"

"Fred."

He stomach rolled. "Is he—"

"Alive." She lifted her face to his. "He's alive and okay."

Tears blurred Nick's eyes as he lifted Steph into his arms and swung her around. "Where is he?"

He lowered her to the ground. "You're not going to believe it?"

She shook her head over and over until he put his hands on each side to stop her. "Tell me what happened."

"Fred's veterinarian called." Her mottled skin was damp with tears, yet happiness glowed in her eyes. "No one will believe this. Somehow Fred found his way there and was hanging outside the building. When the receptionist went out to lunch and came back, he was still there, and she recognized him. Dr. Meade went out, looked at him and said his name. Fred ran up to him and sat."

Nick burst into laughter. "Still obedient even under those conditions. I can't wait for Suzette to have her training." He longed to tell her about Martin and Suzette, but the time didn't seem right. "Ready to go."

"So ready." Tears of joy rolled down her face.

He linked his arm in hers, loving her more and more.

Steph sat on the grass, her arms around Fred's neck and her mind soaring. He smelled so much better since his bath. He'd broken her heart when she saw him—dirty, hungry and sad. When he saw her, he leaped into the air and nearly knocked her over. She didn't care. She loved the crazy dog.

But during the night, she understood even more deeply what Nick had told her about the lost sheep. When Fred disappeared, she did everything to find him—putting up posters, making phone calls, talking with strangers and praying. When she found him, her heart sang and she brought him home. Her love had been so strong that she hadn't given up. She'd told herself so many times to throw away his leash and dishes, but she couldn't. She had hope.

God felt the same about her and rejoiced when she returned to Him. He'd washed her clean with His forgiveness. He didn't punish her for her running away from Him but rejoiced when she returned. Steph wrapped her arms around Fred even tighter.

But Fred's ears perked, and he broke free and ran to the gate.

Steph's heart kicked. Then the gate swung open and Suzette darted into the yard with Nick behind her. Suzette? "Nick, what are you doing?"

He grinned and settled beside her on the grass. "Bringing my dog to play with Fred. It's a welcome home party."

"Your dog?"

She sat, listening as he told her what had happened. "These are the good days you talked about. What's next?"

"Let's celebrate. Today's the Fourth of July." He rose and grasped her hands, pulling her to her feet.

"The fireworks aren't until tonight." The look on his face confused her. "Are we going somewhere?"

"No, but we're celebrating."

She chuckled. "Fred's coming-home party."

"That, too." He pulled out a box of sparklers, handed her one and lit it. She watched the tip sizzle and sparks begin to fly. "Where's yours?"

He held up his finger and put his hand in his pocket. "Steph, my business is suddenly going great. I'm thinking I can afford a house. Then I can take Suzette home, but I feel badly for Fred. What will he do without her?"

She pictured it and didn't like what she saw. "He'll be lonely."

"So will I."

Her nose wrinkled with his puzzling comment.

"I have this idea." He pulled his hand from his pocket and dropped to the ground. "Fred and I would be much happier if we all lived together."

Together? Her mind whirled. "Together, but I don't—"

"And that's why I'm asking you to be my wife." He raised his hand and in his palm was a box.

Steph reeled. She looked at Fred and Suzette sitting beside Nick, their tongues hanging out as if they'd run a mile, and Nick with a grin on his face and eyes twinkling. She looked at his hand, her heart seeming to burst. The sparkler dropped to the ground.

She clasped the box and opened it. Inside sat a magnificent solitaire diamond, between an intricate filigree of gold. She caught her breath as fiery sparks glinted from the ring, greater than any sparkler.

"Do I have to stay down here forever?" Nick sent her a playful, plaintive look.

Her heart swelled with God's gift to her. So many, many gifts. "Fred? Suzette? What do you think?"

Hearing their names, the dogs danced around her feet.

"They like the idea." She grinned. "And so do I."

Nick rose and took her in his arms. His lips touched hers as all her fears fled and happiness filled every empty space.

Nick drew back. "Steph, I love you more than words can say."

"I love you, too. You rescued me once from Martin. You rescued me from my lack of faith, and today you've rescued me again. I'm—"

The last words were silenced by his kiss.

Chapter Fifteen

Saturday, October 10

Steph stepped from the car and gazed at the lovely setting. Today was her wedding day. She'd seen the Community House on Memorial Day when she and Nick had been on the picnic. It had stayed in her mind, and when Nick asked her to marry him, she remembered the beautiful wooded setting and sprawling lawns beneath the mass of oak and maple trees.

Above her the leaves had begun to turn a blend of greens and burnished hues. It mellowed her spirit as she thought back to all that had happened since early May when Nick had leaned against her fence and opened doors she never expected to be unlocked. The burdens of the past years had lifted and vanished. Yes, new problems would arise, but they were solvable. Nick stood by her side and supported her as he'd done since they met. Today the trees added beauty and color to the day just as her life had been colored and made beautiful by Nick's presence.

A soft wind ruffled her hair, and the scent of rich soil and drying leaves followed on the October breeze. The past melted into a new day, and she couldn't wait to be united as one with the man of her dreams, the one who'd opened her heart.

The bright sun dappled the ground as she strode to the gabled entrance. Emily followed, a volunteer to help her with her wedding dress. Steph would always be grateful to her for opening her eyes and helping her understand her husband's death.

But today her new life would begin. *Continue* was a better word. It had begun the day Nick appeared at her fence, his glinting eyes and good looks that ruffled her heart, but even more it was his gentle kindness.

Inside the Community House, she headed for the bride's room. Molly opened her arms when she came through the door. No words needed to be said; the embrace said it all. Molly looked lovely, dressed in a tea-length gown of pastel cinnamon. The dress draped across the front in soft folds, hiding her growing baby bump. Steph's heart leaped seeing her.

Emily and Molly helped her don her gown. The ivory satin flowed from a beaded sweetheart neckline with a ruched bodice to the tea-length skirt adorned with beading. The uneven hemline swept lower in back, adding beauty to the gown. She wished her mother could be there.

But Nick's mother would be with them to celebrate, and Steph had grown to love the woman as a second mother. Her gentle nature and deep love had warmed Steph and given her the family she'd always longed for.

"You're too beautiful for words," Emily said, standing back to admire her gown. "The color is perfect and the beadwork is so delicate. I'd want a dress just like this if I married one day…but then that's only a dream."

Steph drew the young woman into her arms. "We all start with dreams, Emily, but God can make them a reality."

Tears flooded Molly's eyes. "I've waited so long to hear her speak of the Lord in a loving way, and it's all come true. My prayers have been answered."

"My prayers, too." Steph gave her a hug. "And I'm so thrilled you asked me to be godmother to the baby. I'm really honored." Her heart soared for her dear friend, who'd wanted life to be perfect, and now she'd been blessed with a wonderful husband and a baby on the way.

"I wouldn't want anyone else, Steph." Molly brushed tears from her eyes.

Steph grinned, dabbing moisture from her own eyes. "While we're talking about amazing things, you'll never guess who showed up for the wedding."

Molly wrinkled her nose. "I know your dad's here, and Martin's the best man."

Steph grinned. "He's become a different man. He said he was honored to stand up for us."

Emily shook her head. "I'm hoping some of these astounding things happen to me one of these days. You two are an inspiration."

Molly gave her a hug. "Back to guess who's coming to the wedding. You never did answer me. It's not your dad or Martin, so who is it?"

"Who's left?" Her grin grew as she watched Molly's face as she thought.

Finally, Molly's eyes widened. "No. Not Hal."

"Yes, Hal. With an apology and an envelope."

Molly looked at her with one eyebrow raised. "I get the apology, but what was the envelope? A wedding gift."

"Sort of, but it was a check for most of the money he'd stolen." Finally after much prayer, Hal had made a step in the right direction. "It's not the money but the act. I'm so grateful."

"I've told you before. God is good."

Steph clasped Molly's hand. "You never gave up on me and neither has God."

"And neither will Nick, Steph. He's a great guy. You've been so blessed."

A tap sounded on the door, and Emily answered, then closed the door and turned to Steph. "It's time. Your dad's waiting for you."

Steph released a trembling breath, her anticipation rising. "You two better get out there, too."

Molly handed her the flowers that Nick had selected—champagne-colored roses, lemony green hydrangeas and ivy cascading from the bouquet. The sweet scent of roses surrounded her. She cradled the arrangement in her arms as she left the room. Ahead she saw her father. He'd grown much older looking since she'd seen him last, but he'd also grown more gentle. With Hal's attempt to right his wrong, Steph's spirit lifted.

Her father caught her arm, and they held back, waiting for Molly to precede them as she stepped from the doorway and started the lengthy walk down the stone stairs to the patio below where white chairs formed rows for the wedding guests. She'd been touched when some of the longtime dog owners who used her service hinted to be invited, and she could see some of them from the upper level of the grounds.

Molly made her way down the incline, the stair railing wrapped in white ribbon and adorned with an occasional bow. When she reached ground level and made her way to where Martin and Nick waited, Steph and her father stepped outside. She kept her eyes on the stone walkway, fearing she would trip, but her father held her arm with a firm grip.

Beside Martin, Fred and Suzette sat without moving, decked out for the wedding. Fred wore a white bow tie, and Suzette had a white satin bow gracing her well-brushed coat. They had become committed partners just as she and Nick had become.

Nick stood beside his pastor, his gaze sweeping her from head to toe as a smile grew on his face. Her heart filled with joy as she reached the patio, then began her walk down the aisle. A white runner covered the gray stones, and she followed it to the end, then gazed at Nick in his tuxedo with an ivory cummerbund and bow tie, the handsomest man she'd ever known.

Nick's chest tightened as he waited in front of their family and friends, and when Steph came through the door in her amazing gown, his heart kicked up its heels and ran to meet her. Her honey-colored hair hung in long curling waves as she glided toward him on her father's arm. His busy but empty life had become complete when he'd met Steph, and in the past months, his doubts about himself and his ability to be a good husband had faded.

When she reached him, her father moved back,

and Steph stood by his side while the scent of her bouquet encircled them. The pastor's words rose, reminding them of God's desire that man should not be alone. The verse from Ecclesiastes filled his mind. "Two are better than one." Nick agreed. He'd been alone too long. Today his new life would begin and in their new house, away from the memories of Doug's death and a place where Suzette and Fred could romp and not bother anyone.

After they'd exchanged vows and rings, they stood together, eyes locked, and Nick's heart stirred with the blessings he'd been given, a beautiful wife and a lifetime together. With the pastor's announcement, he lowered his lips to hers and drank in the sweetness of joy and laughter, support and trust and, most of all, a shared faith.

When they turned, his mother's face glowed, and gratefulness burst in his chest as the pastor's voice raised. "I give you Mr. and Mrs. Nicholas Davis."

Nick wove his fingers through Steph's, just as their lives were now bound together. They took the first step toward the wonderful life awaiting them. Behind him, he heard the clicking of Fred's and Suzette's nails on the gray stone.

* * * * *

Dear Reader,

Thank you for reading *Groom in Training*. I hope you enjoyed the story. If you related to some of the characters' struggles, I hope it helped you find answers to your own personal questions. Fred's disappearance became a meaningful analogy along with the Scripture of the lost sheep to our own plight as Christians when we become lost and cannot find our way back or when we doubt that God can forgive us. Just as Steph rejoiced at finding Fred, imagine the Lord's jubilation when we return to the fold after straying.

Steph's conflict to understand God's ways is one that many people share. We cannot force others to believe, but we can demonstrate the power of God through our own faith-filled actions, and this form of testimony can be more powerful than our words. Let God's Word shine through you in your daily life. You are His shining witness in a darkened world.

May the Lord bless you as you serve Him.

Gail Gaymer Martin

QUESTIONS FOR DISCUSSION

1. Which character, Steph or Nick, did you relate to the most and why?

2. Why did Nick's past relationship with Cara make him feel like a failure? What is your opinion?

3. How did Nick grow and change?

4. Steph also saw herself as a failure when she didn't recognize her husband's problem. Have you ever felt unable to understand someone in your life? Did you ever feel to blame for their problems, and if so, how did you resolve it?

5. How much are we responsible for our family's difficulties?

6. Suicide is a serious issue in this novel. Has suicide ever touched your life, and how did you deal with it? Did you learn something new about suicide victims and the survivors?

7. What lessons about love and faithfulness can we learn from dogs?

8. What are your favorite themes in this book? How do they relate to you personally?

9. The story shows that Nick's actions reflect his faith. Is this an effective way to help people understand God's love for them?

10. How did Martin grow in this book, and why? Can you relate Martin's experience to your own life or the life of someone you know?

11. Nick's mother played a significant role in this book. In what ways did she affect the story, and how did she provide a catalyst for characters to grow and change?

12. Do you relate personally to any themes or issues in this novel? Can you offer advice to others who are dealing with those same issues?

13. Did you read *Dad in Training,* the book about Molly and Brent? If so, did you enjoy hearing from them again and attending their wedding?

14. Have you learned anything about dog shelters and dogs needing to be adopted? Does it change your attitudes about where you would look for a pet?

Read on for a sneak preview of
KATIE'S REDEMPTION
by Patricia Davids,
the first book in the heartwarming new
BRIDES OF AMISH COUNTRY *series*
available in March 2010
from Steeple Hill Love Inspired.

When a pregnant formerly Amish woman returns
to her brother's house,
seeking forgiveness and a place to
give birth to her child, what she finds
there isn't what she expected.

Please, God, don't let them send me away.

To give her child a home Katie Lantz would endure the angry tirade she expected from her brother. Through it all Malachi wouldn't be able to hide the gloating in his voice.

An unexpected tightening across her stomach made Katie suck in a quick breath. She'd been up since dawn, riding for hours on the jolting bus.

Her stomach tightened again. The pain deepened. Something wasn't right. This was more than fatigue. It was labor.

Breathing hard, she peered through the blowing snow. It wasn't much farther to her brother's farm. Closing her eyes, she gathered her strength.

One foot in front of the other. The only way to finish a journey is to start it.

She sagged with relief when her hand closed over the railing. She was home.

Home. The word echoed inside her mind, bringing with it unhappy memories that pushed aside her relief. Raising her fist, she knocked at the front door. Then she bowed her head and closed her eyes, grasping the collar of her coat to keep the chill at bay.

When the door finally opened, she looked up to meet her brother's gaze.

Katie sucked in a breath and then took a half step back. A tall, broad-shouldered Amish man stood in front of her with a kerosene lamp in his hand and a faintly puzzled expression on his handsome face.

It wasn't Malachi.

To read more of Katie's story, pick up
KATIE'S REDEMPTION
by Patricia Davids,
available March 2010.

Love Inspired® SUSPENSE

RIVETING INSPIRATIONAL ROMANCE

Watch for our new series of
edge-of-your-seat suspense novels.
These contemporary tales
of intrigue and romance
feature Christian characters
facing challenges to their faith...
and their lives!

NOW AVAILABLE IN REGULAR
& LARGER-PRINT FORMATS

Steeple
Hill®

Visit:
www.SteepleHill.com